Geetha
(Gertrude)

SONG
of the
KOEL

— *a novel by* —
GEETHA PATEL

Produced by:

FriesenPress
Suite 300 – 852 Fort Street
Victoria, BC, Canada V8W 1H8

www.friesenpress.com

Distributed to the trade by The Ingram Book Company

DEDICATION

This book is dedicated to my late husband Kersi, who enabled me to widen my mental horizon and open my heart to embrace and respect all religions and spiritual beliefs.

PREFACE

"The Song of the Koel," is a story about the 'Victory of Love'. It takes you on a pleasant and refreshing journey into the lives, beliefs, social expectations and traditions of three women; Maria, Meena and Anna. They believe that "Love is the only freedom in the world because it so elevates the spirit that the laws of humanity and the phenomena of nature do not alter its course." (Kahlil Gibran). This book is a testament to the fact that love can flourish between two human beings, in spite of all the differences and even in the absence of proximity. "Distance is to love like wind is to fire...it extinguishes the small and kindles the great!"

Although, the three women have varied experiences that bring about pain and sorrow in their lives, through the strength of their friendship, they are able to let love in to shape and guide their lives. "In the sweetness of friendship let there be laughter, for in the dew of little things the heart finds its morning and is refreshed." Kahlil Gibran

The book, aims at opening the eyes of the readers, to the many historical facts about India, such as; The Aryan Invasion of India, the beginning of Caste System, the Zoroastrian migration to India, life in the 'Bagh' with the Zoroastrians and the story of Maharaja Digvijay Singh of Nawanagar (Gujarat), who sheltered more than a 1000 Polish Kids after WW11. I hope "Song of the Koel," will educate minds, touch hearts, and move the spirits of the readers

Chapter 1

MARIA

It was a beautiful warm summer day in the year 2004, and Maria was sitting on her deck, sipping coffee. It had a distinct Cherokee flavour, which always invoked her childhood memories of being awakened by the aroma of freshly-brewed coffee. She looked at the clock. There were still three hours before the luncheon meeting with her friends, which was scheduled for the first Monday of every month.

It was a very special day for them. Maria and her friends anticipated it with great eagerness and enthusiasm. It was the day when they could pour their hearts out to each other, share their innermost secrets, and be sure that there would be understanding, celebration, and sympathy—but never ridicule. This was the day of their freedom and confessions. These lunch meetings had brought them closer and strengthened their bond. They were each other's confidants, psychologists, therapists and sources of great strength and inspiration. They met for lunch and stayed till three or even four in the afternoon.

Maria and Anna had been friends for the previous ten years, and Meena was a recent immigrant to Canada who had joined their group by sheer coincidence. Anna had been having coffee, by herself, at the Sherway Garden Mall in Toronto; Meena had joined her simply because she looked very friendly and harmless. During this short coffee time at the mall, Anna recognized that Meena too was a believer in the power of love. Not that these three women were blind and deaf to the struggles and challenges involved in making love work; on the contrary, all three of them had their own share of grief and disappointment. What made them so special was not the absence of struggle, but rather how they managed to overcome their challenges in order to salvage their marriages while sustaining and nourishing their love for their men.

They were of the strong belief that true love started with the meeting of the spirits and souls before it was consummated physically. This love was capable of forgiveness and sacrifice; it could overcome envy, jealousy, and hatred as it elevated the mind, enriched the soul, and liberated the spirit with the unification of the bodies. Though they struggled at times with the natural and base instincts of possessiveness, jealousy, and doubt—and at times had succumbed to them and suffered—they were able to rise above. Furthermore, when Anna came to know that Meena was from Gujarat, something stirred in her heart, and for good reason. Someday she would tell Maria and Meena about it.

By the time they had finished their coffee, Anna had invited Meena for lunch the following Monday at the Red Lobster. Meena, who was so starved for female friendship in this new country, had gladly accepted the invitation.

All three women had unique backgrounds. All three had compelling love stories that consumed, enlightened, and enriched their lives. They had come to understand that love alone was the driving force behind all that was good and all that was evil. When they met, they talked about everything, including their childhoods, their first loves, their marriages, and their hurts. Like Shakespeare, they were in love with love itself. They wondered who among them had really found their soul mate.

Maria was fifty-nine years old; her husband, who was the love of her life, had recently passed away. Her two children were married, and the youngest boy was still with her. Anna was fifty-four, had been widowed ten years earlier, and was just rediscovering love. Meena was forty-three; she had come to Canada only two years earlier because of her second marriage to an Indo-Canadian, after her first husband's death.

Maria wanted to relax on her deck for some time before she got dressed. She looked at her garden with pride. Summer had come early and her garden was filled with the flowers she had planted. The grass was neatly cut by her son, and the birds were at the bird-feeder. She watched the squirrels trying to get to the bird-feed in vain. She had never seen such beautiful birds in India; she didn't even know the names of all of them. She was most fascinated by the hummingbirds—they were so tiny, yet magnificent! The beauty of Canadian flora and fauna mesmerized her. She thought of her life in India. *What a difference!*

Canada was a beautiful and clean country compared to her dirty India—yet she was nostalgic about India, and loved it with all her heart. It was a land where there was "unity amidst diversity and poverty amidst plenty." This was the slogan she had heard growing up in school and at home, and she realized that it was indeed so very true. Indian birds, at least the ones she used to see in South India, were not so colourful, except for the parrots.

Yet, the song of the koel haunted her—sometimes even in her dreams. The eager and insistent male koel sang his mating song—*kuhoo, kuhoo*—and the female promptly responded with her tune—*kik, kik, kik, kik*—in a tone that was almost teasing. She seemed to say, "I know what you want, but you'll only get it when I am ready." They sang two different tunes while communicating the same message. This was their dance of love, in music. This melodious cry had awakened her every morning, especially from March to August. Canadian birds satisfied the sight with their colourful beauty, while the koel churned the hearts of lovers with intense longing.

India, like Canada, was a land of many cultures, languages, and religions, yet they were all bound together by a common and special thread: the love for their motherland. However, the disparity between the rich and the poor in India was greater than any country on Earth. There was a belief and perception that the poor were poor because of their Karma, in their last birth. This belief by mainstream Hindus was the reason for the poor Hindu's acceptance of his fate and the rich Hindu's apathy towards him.

Maria Rose was born in 1945 to Roman Catholic parents who were both Gaud Saraswat Brahmins by ancestry. Her father was always proud of this and never let them forget it. Their ancestral last name was *Prabhu*—and her father always reminded them of that, too. Brahmins (the priest class) were the highest caste in the hierarchical caste system of India. Contrary to the common belief by many Hindus (especially in the north) that all Christians were converted from the untouchables, there were a lot of Brahmins who were also converted to Christianity, especially in Goa. The Mangaloreans were those who left Goa and travelled to Mangalore; they had done this because they wanted to keep the old Hindu customs and dress.

During Maria's childhood, Christian women (once married) always wore a sari; the Mangalorean Christians also preserved and followed some of the Hindu customs of marriage and the celebration of the Harvest Festival—unlike the Goan Christians. This festival was celebrated on the same day as the Nativity of Mary. Only vegetarian food was eaten on that day, along with tender grains from the new shoots of rice. This festival was so esteemed among the Mangalorean Christians that it superseded Christmas and Easter in importance. During this festival, families reunited from distant lands to celebrate. In the town of Mangalore, where Maria came from, all of the families knew each other—and all knew who were the Brahmin converts and who were not. This could be discerned by their last names and by the way they spoke their mother tongue. Many in Mangalore, had started using their ancestral Brahmin last names.

Maria's aunt had told her that in a small village called Udyawar (which was near Mangalore), there used to be two churches. The upper church was for the Brahmin converts and the lower church for the lower-caste converts. This story troubled Maria. *If Christianity is casteless, then how come the Catholics are so hung up on the caste system even after conversion?* She wondered. Maria had no answer to this question. Some things were just accepted as part of the tradition and custom. On her last trip to Mangalore, she had heard from one of her Hindu Brahmin professors that he had written a paper titled "Conversion to Christianity in India" and had discovered that some of the Brahmins did convert to Christianity as they found answers to some of the questions they were struggling with, in their own faith. He had promised Maria that on her next trip he would let her read his completed paper.

Maria's dad, Pedro, was a hardworking and honest man who loved his job and the coffee plantation he managed. The diligence with which he tended to the coffee plants on his supervisory rounds, chopping the shoots which were missed by the workers, was a sight to behold. He loved those plants almost as if they were his children. Maria remembered him dressed in khaki shorts and knee-length socks, with cap and a cane in hand, getting ready for his work. What a handsome man he was, with a smile which displayed his perfect teeth. All Maria's mother's cousins flirted with him openly, but he had eyes only for his virtuous, beautiful, and devoted wife. He walked a lot during a day, up and down the slopes, and was fit for his age. It was a real shame that this active man had to die of "King's Disease" which is called Lou Gehrig's disease in North America. It deteriorated his muscles, making him unable to walk during the last days of his life.

Pedro was also very fond of politics and kept abreast of world news. He read the English as well as the vernacular newspapers and informed his older children and his wife what was going on in the world. Maria remembered his delight when Eichmann was caught, and his admiration for Moshe Dayan, the commander-in-chief of the Israeli Army. He admired Moshe Dayan not only for his brilliant military tactics, but also for his humane side. He was so fascinated at his ability to defeat the Arabs that surrounded the tiny land of Israel that he was convinced that God alone must have helped him to win this war. Maria remembered the smiling face of her father as he praised the military expertise of this great man. She remembered him as the man with a patch on one eye. Though Maria was still too young to understand the full implications of the war between Israel and the surrounding Arabs at that time, her father had explained it to her later.

Maria had learnt more about Moshe Dayan later in her life through the internet. On a website at palestineremembered. com, she had found a page titled "Moshe Dayan—A Brief Bibliography and Quotes." Two of Moshe Dayan's quotes had impressed her and touched her heart: the first he had uttered in 1950, saying, "Using the moral yardstick mentioned by [Moshe Sharett], I must ask: Are we justified in opening fire on the [Palestinian] Arabs who cross [the border] to reap the crops they planted in our territory; they, their women, and their children? Will this stand up to moral scrutiny?...Arabs cross to collect the grain that they left in the abandoned villages, and we set mines for them and they go back without an arm or a leg...but I know no other method of guarding the borders..."1 Maria then knew how he must have struggled with the moral aspect of planting land mines in the land which once belonged to the Palestinians. She could understand her father's admiration for this man with a compassionate heart. Moshe Dayan truly lamented that he did not know any other way of guarding the Israeli borders. In India, they would say that Moshe Dayan was doing his Dharma or duty as a commander-in-chief—and all is well when one does his Dharma.

The second quote by Moshe Dayan increased her respect for this great man; at the funeral of an Israeli farmer killed by a Palestinian Arab in 1956, he said, "...Let us not today fling accusation at the murderers. What cause have we to complain about their fierce hatred towards us? For eight years now, they sit in their refugee camps in Gaza, and before their eyes we turn into our homestead the land and villages in which they and their forefathers have lived. We should demand blood not from the [Palestinian] Arabs of Gaza, but from ourselves."2

---

1   Benny Morris, *Righteous Victims* (Vintage Books, 2001), page 275.

2   Avi Shlaim, *Israel and the Arab World* (W. W. Norton & Company, 2001), page 101.

Maria was grateful to her father for giving her a head start in world politics and history.

Maria's dad was a great storyteller. The simplest story was told with so much emotion and suspense that children as well as adults loved to hear them. Many of them were about his hunting experiences, ghosts, encounters with wild animals, and killing of tigers. In those days, the tigers were not deemed endangered species; the killing and displaying of their skins on the walls of homes was both British and Indian sport. However, tigers were not killed till they crossed the line from the jungle to the inhabited areas and attacked their cattle. Once this happened, the tiger was considered dangerous and was killed.

Killing the tiger was another production by itself. First, they had to make sure the path of the tiger through its paw prints. Then, three to four men went before sunset and perched themselves on trees, with lights bound to their heads so that their hands were free for shooting; this ensured their safety. Once the sun set, they waited for the arrival of the tiger. Maria's father would tell his children that when the tiger started coming through the forest, the birds and the monkeys started screeching. This was their clue to get their guns ready and to search for the tiger with their headlights. Once they spotted the tiger, all lights would be focussed on the tiger's eyes, to make it literally blind. Then, each of the hunters would shoot at the tiger till it was dead. Only the vegetarian Hindus did not take part in such a violent sport, especially on the coffee plantations. Maria's father had taught her so much about hunting and its inherent dangers that she could have been a hunter herself. Some of those stories still remained etched in her memory. One such story involved her dad's encounter with the tiger as a teenager.

When Maria's dad was about sixteen years old, his mother sent him to the nearby town to fetch something. The way to the little shop was through the jungle. She warned him that it was dangerous to return after sunset. Pedro, being a typical teenager, met up with his friends in town. By the time he realized that it was getting dark, it was too late. He bought the stuff his mother had sent him for, and quickly made his way back home. Being the month of June and monsoon season, he carried an umbrella, which he was using as a cane. As he walked through the forest in the serene silence of dusk, his umbrella made a distinct sound as it hit the ground. It was getting darker by the minute and he was getting a bit nervous, as there was no telling what danger lurked in the forest.

Suddenly, Pedro saw two round balls shining in the dark; instinctively, he knew those were the eyes of the tiger. For a second, their gaze met—the predator and the prey. Blood curdled in his veins and he almost froze! Seconds seemed like an eternity. In his intuitive wisdom, he decided to continue his journey in the same direction and at the same pace. Thus, he walked with his umbrella, continuing to make the same rhythmic sound as it hit the ground, though his heart pounded with fear. He dared not look back, nor did he run. The minutes it took to reach home were the scariest minutes of his life. Only after he was safely home, did he venture to see if the tiger had followed him. He was glad it had not. Never again did he walk through the jungle after dark. Maria could still feel the tension as he was telling his children this story.

After telling this story, her father had asked Maria and her siblings to tell him why the tiger neither attacked nor followed him. When they could not give him the right answer, he had explained to them the reason.

"The tiger didn't perceive me as a threat as I neither stopped nor ran. Secondly, a tiger attacks human beings only when he is hungry or wounded and, as a result, incapable of running fast enough to catch his prey."

"What if he was hungry, but not wounded?"

"It is said that a tiger who has never tasted human flesh will not attack a harmless human being. Unlike humans, animals do not kill for pleasure, but only for food or self-protection."

Maria had narrated this story to all the students in her teaching carrier and all of them, no matter what their age, had loved it.

Since her dad was a manager of a coffee plantation, Maria and her siblings were all placed in boarding schools in the nearby towns. They went home to their parents only on Christmas and summer holidays. She paused to think how many years of her life she had really spent at home if she did not count the holidays. It was exactly nine years of her entire life! This had made her and her siblings, especially the older ones, very tough and independent. They had to learn to live with others and get along with them if they did not want to be bullied. They had survived without getting scarred or damaged. These skills of survival among students with different temperaments, religions, and beliefs had helped them in their journeys through life.

Maria's mother, Lucy, was a product of the British Raj. It was evident in the way she dressed, carried herself, and the manners—especially table manners she insisted upon, which were all learned from the English rulers. "Don't talk with your mouth full; don't eat with your mouth open—only pigs eat with their mouths open. Don't polish your plate to look like you have no food, and don't put your elbows on the table," were her daily commandments. They were also not allowed to leave the table until everyone had finished their food. Her father was usually the first to leave the table. Maria's mother insisted that all children were to come for breakfast in a presentable manner. Maria, being the eldest, was responsible to ensure that all her siblings had brushed their teeth, changed their night clothes, and combed their hair before her father came to the breakfast table.

Maria's mother was the daughter of a coffee planter and it was unthinkable that a daughter of a coffee planter would marry an employee in another plantation. In that respect, their union was rare. Pedro was from a village and was a farmer's son before he became a manager in his uncle's plantation. He was not brought up the way Maria's mother was, but he did not interfere with his wife's rules for the children. In fact, he liked her discipline and manners, as he himself was a very disciplined man.

As tiny as Maria's mother was, she not only managed the servants and the household, but also looked after the children and their education whenever they were home for the holidays. Maria still remembered how her father made her mother read his letters before making a good copy, as her English was better than his. He loved her very much and consulted her opinion in all important things. Many times, he openly said that she was all he ever wanted in a woman and a wife.

Her mother was a petite woman, yet she managed her six children with an iron hand. Maria remembered the routine they followed during the few years she spent at home. From the time they got up till they went to bed, the children followed a kind of timetable. There was time for study, time for play, time for prayers, and time for bed, which was strictly adhered to during school days. There were two days in a week for washing the long hair Maria and her sisters had. There was school even on Saturday till noon. Sunday was a day assigned to church, relaxation, and visiting family. Maria's mother was a walking book of sayings and quotations. Her famous quotations were, "Order leads to God," "East or west, home is the best," and "Cleanliness is next to godliness." Her mother rattled away the sayings and quotations in English, while Maria and her siblings were studying in the vernacular medium of instruction and speaking in their own mother tongue at home. As a result, the children did not understand the full meaning of these English sayings and quotations, though they understood the gist. When her mother said, "Stitch in time saves nine," Maria took the literal meaning and started mending and darning her dad's socks as soon as her holidays started.

Maria had done the very same with her own children. The saying, "Like mother, like daughter," proved to be very true.

As soon as Maria had finished her Bachelor of Education, she had travelled to Bombay, a city of dreams. It was the year 1965, and by the age of twenty, Maria had her B.A. and B.Ed. degrees. She had left the small town to find a job and live independently in a reputed women's hostel—and find her own man.

Bombay was the greatest culture shock she had ever experienced to that date. She was shocked to see those tall buildings, and moreover, the crowds of people wherever she went. Accommodations had previously been arranged and a teaching job was also lined up for her. The rest of her friends were also teachers; they too had secured jobs in good schools. All was done through correspondence. Maria reached this flashy city on a Thursday and had a few days to organize before school started on Monday.

The church, tailor, pharmacy, doctor, market, and a shoe repair stall were all within close range to her hostel. Once she got settled in this big, crowded city and her teaching job—which was in a convent school nearby—time seemed to pass very quickly. Maria sent some money home every month after paying her hostel fees (keeping a few rupees for her own needs) as her mother needed any extra help she could get. She would have been happy if Maria had stayed in the town and worked there, as that would have saved money (which could have been given to her mother), but Maria wanted adventure away from home. Come to think of it, she was a selfish person by Indian standards.

Her uncle, who also lived in Bombay, came to see Maria at the hostel, and invited her to spend Sundays at his place. Her aunt cooked such delicious food; after a week of insipid food at the hostel, it was a real treat. She went regularly to her uncle's place and spent whole Sundays there. However, she never spent the nights there for many reasons. Her uncle lived in a very small apartment—smaller than a bachelor pad—with his four children. That one room had a stove in one corner and a little place for a shower in the other. The shower was also used to clean dishes and wash clothes. The rest of the place was used as a dining room, living room, and bedroom. Her uncle had improvised extra space by building an attic on the top of this stove/shower area, where the kids slept. Maria could not even begin to imagine how, in that meagre space with absolutely no privacy, they had managed to create four kids.

The washrooms were outside and they were common to the tenants of the building. These were filthy with no septic tank. There was just a hole were men, women, and children defecated. This was manually cleaned by the untouchable women, who were beneath the four Indian castes, and that was their job. These were things Maria and others took for granted growing up, and it troubled her soul later in life.

During the non-monsoon season, some boys slept on the open terrace with meagre bedding. Maria had heard some juicy stories about what happened there; she was told that rarely the girls also slept up on the terrace. There were two different sides for the boys and girls. However, it was rumoured that sometimes in the dark of the night, some boys and girls snuck next to each other. In a society where open dating was forbidden by most households, the young girls and boys had to invent ways of relieving their sexual tension. The desires and heat of youth combined with the darkness of the night contributed to the daring and adventurous risks. Sometimes, these encounters did end up in marriage, but most of the time they remained the secrets of the night. When Maria had heard some of these stories floating around, she understood why her uncle never let his girls go up to the terrace.

Though Maria was also from India, she was equally appalled by the living conditions of her uncle and his family, because in her town of Mangalore everyone had a small or big house with fruit trees in their yards. There were no apartments, nor were there such poor living conditions there. Bombay, on the other hand, was rated as having some of the most expensive real estate in the world. As a result, people couldn't afford bigger places unless they had ancestral property, were businessmen, professionals, or their children were working in the Middle East or North America. Maria was saddened to see homeless people living in large pipes, which were close to the very posh buildings where the rich lived. Besides the class system based on wealth and education, India was also plagued by the caste system.

Maria, being an Indian History major, was well aware of the historical fact that the Aryans invaded India somewhere around 1000 B.C. They were nomads from the Caucasian Mountains who settled in the planes of River Indus and its tributaries, as the soil was fertile and the weather was moderate. Since they came to India through the Hindu Kush

Mountains, they occupied the north by defeating the peace-loving native Dravidians and pushing them to the south. The Dravidians were dark-skinned and short, and were a very intelligent people with a sophisticated civilization. The Indus Valley Civilization had been flourishing when the Aryans came to India. The caste system started after their arrival, mainly because of their belief in the superiority of their race. It was originally based on colour or *varna*, where the light-skinned Aryans were assigned the three top castes and the Dravidians the lowest caste. It was a complex social structure similar to the Indo-European tribal divisions of Priests, warriors and commoners. Priests were the Brahmins, warriors were the Kshatriyas, and the commoners were the Vaishyas. It is believed that originally these castes could be interchanged by a Brahmin's son choosing to be a warrior, or a warrior choosing to be a common merchant. However, as time went by, these castes became rigid and could only be acquired by birth. A male did not lose his caste even if he married a woman of lower caste, but a female did. Furthermore, through "The Laws of Manu" written in the Vedas (the ancient Aryan scriptures), caste system obtained religious credence and authenticity. These top three castes started being known as "twice born" while the Shudras were known as "once born". They were the outcasts and the untouchables. Their jobs were cleaning the feces of human beings, dealing with the carcasses of dead animals and such. Maria was glad that Gandhiji had done a lot to eradicate this menace. He ate with the untouchables and renamed them as *Harijan*, or children of God. In spite of all this progress, caste system and the ill-treatment of the Shudras or Dalits continues to exist and thrive in some villages in India.

Maria looked at the clock. She had twenty minutes to get ready and go for lunch with her friends. Her mind had travelled far back in time. She felt fascinated with the capacity of the mind to remember things of the past, by a mere sight, sound, or touch. She got dressed quickly and left the house.

Chapter 2
MEENA

Meena was a recent arrival to Canada, and was faced with the dual challenge of adapting to a new country and a new marriage. She was a Gujarati, which meant that she was from the state of Gujarat, like Gandhi. She was born in 1961 in Surat (or Suryapur), which is situated on the banks of river Tapti. Surat, an important trading centre, was esteemed because of Mahatma Gandhi. The two important places in Surat connected with the "Freedom Fight" were Bardoli and Dandi. The Dandi March was organized by Mahatma Gandhi as a protest against the British for the tax they levied on the Indians. This March was launched on March 12, 1930 as an act of civil disobedience against the British. Bardoli was also famous because of the farmer's movement, which was another strike, or *Satyagrah*, launched by Gandhi under the leadership of Sardar Vallabhbhai Patel, a famous freedom fighter who was also from Gujarat. It was no wonder, then, that Meena was extremely patriotic. Besides its connection to the freedom movement of India, Surat was also famous for its magnificent cotton textiles, diamond cutters, and embroidered brocade saris of intricate designs woven with gold and silver threads.

Meena's father was a textile merchant and quite well off. He had great expectations for his only daughter. He encouraged her to study as much as she wanted, and when she completed her C.A., he wanted her to marry into a family where her talents and education would be appreciated and used. They were Vaishyas by caste, which is the merchant class of India. Great entrepreneurs have emerged from this caste of Indians.

Meena's father was a self-made man. His beginnings were quite humble, yet through perseverance, hard work, and shrewd business sense, he had attained success. He loved his wife and daughter and wanted the best for them. He also helped his siblings in their education or the starting of a new business. Her mother was married when she was just nineteen and had devoted her life to her husband and child. Meena remembered her keeping a picture of her husband with the pictures of gods, praying every day for his long life and prosperity. Meena would sometimes laugh at her mother and say, "When did Dad become God?"

"Haven't you heard the phrase *Pathidev*? It literally means 'Husband God.'"

"Hope my husband won't expect me to worship him, too."

"You are wrong, Meena. Your father does not expect me to do this. I do it for my own reasons. What life will I have without him? Don't you know and haven't you seen the plight of women who have lost their husbands?"

Meena had seen the life of her aunt who had lost her husband. She had lost all power of making decisions for her children. Her brother-in-law had taken charge of her and her children's lives. She could not participate in many festivals and could not wear colourful clothes. Meena had also seen

changes for the better among the younger educated generation and was glad for that.

Meena was the only child and hence was pampered by her
parents. Her mother was suffering from a rheumatic heart,
and therefore was advised by her doctor not to conceive again
as it would put her life at great risk. Meena studied in a convent
school run by the nuns and then studied accounting at Baroda
University. As per the custom, she was married, as soon as she
had finished her C.A., to a businessman called Deepak. That
was the year 1984. Deepak's family was quite broadminded,
especially the men. Her father-in-law was quite happy that
someone from the family could manage the accounts for their
business. Meena was glad that things were changing in India;
more and more women were entering the workforce with the
blessing of their parents and in-laws.

Deepak was a handsome man who was a bit reserved by
nature. Two days before the wedding, her sister-in-law, Shaila,
called her for a chat at a nearby restaurant. Meena was glad
for the opportunity.

"Meena, I'm glad you are going to be my sister-in-law.
Everyone in the family is happy with this match."

"I am so glad they are. My parents are very happy with
Deepak, too."

"I am sure Deepak has told you about Gita."

"Who is Gita?"

"It was the girl who was his classmate in college. He was
completely smitten by her, and they used to meet secretly.
When her parents came to know about it, they were upset
and forced her to stop seeing Deepak. She was a Brahmin."

"What did Deepak say?"

"Deepak, though very upset, had no choice. He realised
that there was no point in continuing unless they were ready

to elope, and that was not what either of them wanted. Deepak was so much in love with her that I wonder if he has completely forgotten her."

Meena's heart sank. Shaila was pushing it too far. Did she want to ruin Meena's life? Meena had to gather all her composure to continue the conversation with Shaila. She was relieved when Shaila had changed the subject. After a few minutes of chatting about the jewellery and saris for the wedding, they parted.

Meena had met Deepak a few times before their engagement, but he had not mentioned anything about this other girl, Gita. In fact, she had asked Deepak if he had any girlfriends, and he had cleverly changed the subject. Meena was upset. She wanted to confront Deepak and ask him the reason for his non-disclosure. Somehow, she could not find the time to meet him before the wedding as there were too many ceremonies to which she had to be subjected. The most important one was *Pithi (Haldi)*, where the bride and groom, in their separate houses, have a paste of sandalwood, rosewater, and haldi (turmeric) applied on the body. This is a ritual which not only cleanses the body, but also makes the skin smooth, blemish-free, and radiant.

Meena sat there while the womenfolk sang songs and applied the haldi on her face, hands, arms, knees, and feet. Young girls giggled, and the older women sang songs with messages and advice to the young bride. This was supposed to be a happy occasion. Meena, however, was deep in her thoughts. She knew that the bride and the groom had to refrain from seeing each other till the wedding day. When was she going to ask Deepak about his former girlfriend? The only alternative left was to confront Deepak on her wedding night. Though she felt that it was neither the time nor place for such a confrontation, she went against her instincts and decided to settle this matter before they consummated their marriage. *If Deepak is still in love with Gita, then the marriage consummation can wait,* thought Meena.

It was Meena's wedding night, and Deepak came to their bed, which was strewn with rose petals. There she sat in all her wedding finery. There was mehndi on her feet and hands, and she was veiled, as per custom. Deepak came and sat on the bed and slowly lifted her veil. She looked so beautiful that he could not take his eyes off her. His heart was racing. There was love and devotion in his eyes. On the other hand, Meena looked unhappy. She did not bow her head low to avoid his adoring gaze as she was supposed to. On the contrary, she looked straight at him and asked him why he had not told her about his girlfriend, and asked him if he still loved her.

Deepak was so taken aback by this, that he withdrew his hand from her veil and stared at her. "Did you think this was the best time for you to ask this question? I did not tell you, because I wanted to forget all about her, and start a new life with you. Now, I am so upset with your outburst that I am going to leave you to think about it. Thanks for ruining our first night."

Saying this, he went to the washroom, changed his clothes, and slept on the floor with a blanket and pillow.

What have I done? Meena thought. Yet she could not touch him without knowing the truth. She did not know what to do. She knew this was not right, yet she had no other course of action. She lay down on her bed alone, awake and miserable, trying to get some sleep, but she could not. By morning her eyes were swollen with crying. She was glad she was near-sighted and needed glasses. Though she usually wore contacts, she decided to wear her glasses, which were slightly tinted. To her great relief, the members of the family thought she looked tired because of the activities of the night. They teased her about it. *Why did my sister-in-law have to tell me about Gita? What purpose has it served, except place a wedge between Deepak and I?* Meena thought. She was really angry with herself, Deepak, and her sister-in-law. She did not know who to blame. *Sooner or later, he will come to me,* thought Meena.

Many a night Meena cried herself to sleep. She could not confide in anyone. It would be considered her fault if their marriage was not consummated. The elders would conclude that something was wrong with her. Though Meena knew that this was a wrong line of thinking, she would not be able to change things that were so deeply entrenched in their brains. It would take at least two more generations of educated women to bring about the required change in perception. Meena hoped that Deepak would forgive her for ruining their wedding night.

Deepak did not bring up the topic of Gita again, and neither did Meena. He was angry and upset at first. As the months went by, he started admiring the resilience of his wife and her dedication to her duty as a wife in all other respects. She attended to his clothes and packed his lunch every day, just like the older sister-in-law. He did not know how to approach her after such a long time of being distant. Both were waiting for the other to take the first step. His heart warmed up to her, but Meena had no way of knowing what he felt for her, unless he expressed it. They continued to talk politely to each other about things related to business. There was no other talk between them. This was not the marriage Meena had dreamt about. It was getting very hard to continue this pretence. If they were alone, she could have talked to him openly. They could have fought if need be and solved the problem. Under these circumstances, the problem was just brewing within themselves. She did not know what to do. Living in a joint or extended family was not helping the matter. Besides, being the very busy months of the year, their honeymoon was also postponed. Meena felt helpless and exhausted.

Days turned into weeks and weeks into months, but neither Deepak nor Meena took the first step towards reconciliation. Meena found out that there was a Jain monastery for nuns, where they lead a celibate life. She thought it would be better to join those nuns, rather than go back home where she really had no place once she was married. Dating and second marriage was also not easy in those days. After months of this silence, Meena packed her bags for the ashram, and was about to leave with a note when Deepak saw her.

"What are you doing? Where are you going, Meena?"

"Since you do not love me and have no desire to even talk to me, I have decided to go to the Jain Ashram. You will be a free man to choose a woman you can love."

He was horrified, not only because the whole family would know their story, but also because he realized that he had failed in his Dharma (duty) as a husband. In his anger and guilt, he had neglected his young wife and had not thought of her needs, wants, or dreams. He had to answer her question with all honesty and convince her that he loved no one other than Meena. She had a right to know and, in fact, he should have told her this story about Gita before he married her.

"I am really sorry, Meena. In spite of my stubbornness, you have been a good wife by keeping up appearances in front of the members of the extended family, and have not discussed our problems with anyone. I apologize for my callous behaviour. Can you please forgive me and give our marriage a second chance? To answer your question: yes, I was in love with Gita for two years. We were intimate only to a certain extent, and never crossed the line. She would never have adjusted to my family as you have done. Furthermore, she wanted me to start a new business or go abroad, which was unthinkable for me. My family business needs me, and I did not want to leave. Secondly, she was a Brahmin, and would have found it difficult to adjust. You are a special woman—admirable and beautiful. I have fallen in love with you, but had no guts to approach you after such a long time."

Saying this, he came close to her. When he saw the softened expression on her face, he hugged her close and held her in his arms for a long time. Meena felt blood rushing to her face, and emotion flooded her heart. As a good Hindu wife, she agreed to stay; she unpacked her things, and decided to give their marriage and her love a second chance.

That night, when he came into their room, she sat on her bed dressed in her wedding finery; that was the night they consummated their marriage. He was repentant, tender, and loving. When he touched his beautiful and patient wife, all his desires, which had been kept in check, burst forth with true adoration and love. That night, they vowed to be always open and true to each other, no matter what. He took her in his arms and told her that she was a good wife, that he loved and admired her, and that he was truly a lucky man.

That day was a turning point in their lives. Deepak ripped all the pictures of scantily-clad Indian actresses he had in their room and replaced them with only their wedding picture and pictures of the goddess of wealth (Lakshmi) and goddess of knowledge (Saraswathi). They knew that he should have gotten rid of the pictures before his wedding, but somehow he did not. Meena, like most Indian wives of that time, had said nothing. Deepak also arranged for prayer meetings for couples once a week as Meena had wanted. That day was the true dawn of her married life. From then on, her marriage and their love for each other bloomed with all its glory and beauty. Meena soon became pregnant and delivered two boys within three years. Producing an heir was a coveted thing for an Indian woman, and this raised her status as a wife and mother in the family. Even her mother-in-law treated her with a renewed respect. The older sister-in-law also had a boy; her boy was the oldest of the three, which also secured her hierarchical place in the joint family. It was a winning situation for all.

Meena had been living in this extended family for a few years, and had quickly learnt to adapt. Though her mother-in-law originally had preferred her elder daughter-in-law because she was a housewife and did all the cooking, Meena did not hold it against her. Meena knew that her mother-in-law was old-fashioned and did not like women working. She gradually earned the respect of both her sister-in-law and her mother-in-law by showing them that a woman can be as important and competent as any man. They were glad that Meena could do what they could not, and started giving her the love and admiration she deserved. The family business was doing well, and Deepak was a busy man who worked long hours. There were times when Meena resented the long hours of work, and sometimes even doubted his faithfulness, especially when he got home in the wee hours of the morning. Though this was rare, it made her terribly upset. One day, she decided to get to the bottom of it. She was not going to be in the dark anymore.

"You are late again, Deepak. Don't tell me you had a meeting or you had to meet a client at 1:00 a.m. You should tell me if you are having an affair."

"No, Meena. I swear on my children that I am truly not having an affair. I was with some friends."

"Are these friends married or single? Which decent married man stays out with his friends so late? You are not telling me the whole truth, Deepak. Didn't we promise to be truthful to each other? Whatever it is, tell me please. I love you. Didn't I bear your distance and silence for months?"

Deepak felt guilty for breaking his promise of being open and honest. He had to tell her if he did not want her to think that he was having an affair. Meena was confused. If he was cheating on her, how could he have the energy to make love to her no matter what time he came home? Meena could not understand what was happening.

"If you must know the truth, here it is. I am embarrassed to tell you that some of my friends and I watch porn movies. There are no women present there. We don't bring our wives, lest we offend them. I was curious about these movies at first. My college friend, Ajit, has come from the U.S.A. and we met at his house to see these movies. Now we meet to have foreign scotch and talk about life in the U.S. Ajit will be leaving soon, Meena."

Meena was relieved that he was not having an affair. According to the way she was brought up and the concessions that were being made for the behaviour of men, watching a movie was nothing, and not even as bad as drinking and smoking. As long as he was hers, and this was just a temporary thing, she could live with it. Out of the two things he had told her, the drinking bothered her more. None in her family drank liquor.

Something that western kids had access to at an early age was not easily available in Gujarat, India in 1985. Hence, it was a novelty to these men at that time.

"Oh my God! I am so relieved."

Meena had never seen a porn movie in her life and did not bother to know the details. All she knew was that they were about sex. On the other hand, she had read the Kamasutra and was familiar with different sexual poses. Sex was never considered wrong or immoral as long as it was within the boundaries of marriage. Ancient India regarded sex as almost sacred. Many temples had carvings of naked gods and goddesses in the most erotic poses.

Deepak was happy that the cat was out of the bag at last, and was also pleased that Meena understood.

"Thank you for understanding, Meena. Please know that you are the only woman I love, and if in your anger you cut me into pieces, every piece will cry out your name."

"Don't be so dramatic, Deepak. I will never hurt you. I am glad this drinking and watching of movies will stop once Ajit returns to the U.S.A. Did he come to get a wife?"

"Yes, he did, but he is returning without one, as he has not found his match. His parents, as well as the match-makers, are quite disappointed."

"Please remember that trust is the most important factor in a married life, and honesty alone can build that trust."

Deepak took her in his arms and kissed her with tenderness and love. He was indeed a very lucky man. Then he whispered in her ear, "No matter where I get my appetite, I will always eat at home."

She understood what he meant, and they both laughed.

Meena remembered the story of Shah Jehan, one of the great Mogul kings who ruled India and built the beautiful Taj Mahal in memory of his wife, Mumtaz Mahal. It was said that Mumtaz had many miscarriages; at one point, the doctor had warned the couple not to engage in sex, because if she ever became pregnant again, she would die in childbirth. The king was still young; Mumtaz knew that he needed to satisfy his carnal needs, so she sent him a girl on a regular basis. However, she not only made sure that the girl was not very beautiful, but also that the same girl was never sent twice, in order to prevent the king from falling in love. Mumtaz, in her wisdom, knew that love and sex were two different things for men. The king, who was deeply in love with his wife, was unable to stay away from her, in spite of the young girls; their passionate encounter resulted in Mumtaz getting pregnant again, and then dying in childbirth.

The king was said to have become so distraught by her death that he became almost suicidal. He blamed himself, and then built the magnificent Taj Mahal in honour of their undying love for each other. When Shah Jehan was later imprisoned by his own son and kept captive in the "Red Fort" or Lal Quila, he spent his last days watching the Taj Mahal, which was clearly visible from his death bed. When he died, he was made to rest next to Mumtaz. This story had proved to Meena that love and lust were two different things; she realized that Deepak truly loved her and that perhaps those movies he watched had simply satisfied his curiosity.

Deepak and Meena had a special bond of love and under-standing. They were emotionally and sexually compatible—so much so that most of her friends envied their love. After more than ten years of being married, they remained very much in love. Even her sister-in-law once had asked her, "What magic have you done to your husband that he is always so affection-ate and attentive and has that look of love and admiration for you? I wish my husband was the same to me."

Meena smiled. "I am sure your husband also loves you," she said. "Some are introverts and do not show their affection and admiration. Deep down, he loves you and is very proud of your excellent cooking and how you manage the house-hold. Now that Ma is getting old, you have been taking on all the responsibilities. That is admirable, Shaila. As for Deepak and myself, we understand each other's needs and wants, and we are mentally and spiritually compatible."

"What about sexually?" Maria's sister-in-law had asked her in confidence.

"That too," Meena had answered with a smile. It was their secret, and now she had told it to her sister-in-law. The chemistry was still there, and though the intensity had decreased, Meena was going to keep the fire burning.

Meena and Deepak were at a very good place both in their business and marriage. She could not have asked for anything more. When things go too well, one has to be prepared for things to change. Nothing remains too good or bad for too long. There is always a turn of events. Ecstasy or agony is both fleeting. Joy and sorrow, too, are short-lived. So was the case in Meena's life.

One morning, Deepak complained of pain in his chest, and Meena saw the drops of cold sweat on his forehead.

"Meena, aren't these signs of a heart attack? Didn't you read the book I brought few days ago and tell me the symptoms? Call the doctor, Meena."

She knew at once that he had suffered a heart attack, and when he threw up, she was dead certain of it. She called the family doctor and the ambulance at the same time. The doctor arrived first. He tried his best, but before her very eyes, her Deepak breathed his last, even before the ambulance arrived.

Meena's whole life came crashing down. She felt an immense loss within her heart and soul. Her husband of thirteen years was gone forever. She would never forget that year, month, or hour—almost noon on January 20, 1997. It not only devastated and saddened her, but she also felt guilty for not looking after him properly. She felt that she must not have been a really good wife. How else could he have died so young? One of Deepak's aunts had also commented on her ability as a wife. Perhaps she was right. *Being a professional, I must not have given my husband the full attention that stay-at-home wives are capable of*, thought Meena. She felt sad, helpless, and very lonely. Then she remembered what her mother had once told her:

"Life is a mystery. Nothing remains the same. Enjoy life, and give all you have when life is good; don't be afraid to suffer when sufferings come—they too shall pass. Pain and pleasure are the two sides of the same coin, and time heals the greatest wounds."

Meena's parents came at once to be with their daughter in her grief. Their presence was a great help and support for Meena. As per the custom, Meena wore a white sari for the three months after her husband died. The old Hindu custom would have been to break her glass bangles, erase the red mark from her forehead and hair parting, shave her head, and wear only a white sari for the rest of her life. This was done to stop the widow from looking attractive to other men. Once a woman became a widow, she had no right to look good for anyone else. One day, her mother-in-law came to her, gave her a hug, and cried. Meena knew that a mother's grief was more than that of a wife's. No mother would ever want to lose her child.

"Meena, you don't have to wear the white sari from now on. The three months are over. Wear whatever colour you want and, if you feel like it, put a *bindi* (mark) on your forehead. We have no objection. You made my son happy, and we want to see you happy."

Meena was touched by her mother-in-law's words. She had indeed married into a very nice household. Her parents were equally happy to know of the understanding and freedom their daughter was enjoying in her home. They were also glad that the customs were not so rigid among the educated Indians, especially their son-in-law's family. Meena continued to work for the family business. Her in-laws invested the due share of

Deepak in his two sons' names and looked after the expenses of Meena and the boys. They also paid Meena decent wages for her work and treated her with great love and respect.

Meena was only thirty-six years old at the time of her husband's death. She concentrated on her work and time passed by. There were times when she missed Deepak very much, and during those times she spoke to him as if he were there sitting beside her and listening to her. This always helped, as Deepak would give her, an answer to her question in some strange manner, and her depression and loneliness would be dramatically eased. One day she was so distraught and lonely that she questioned Deepak as to why he had left her, and she sobbed with so much pain. All of a sudden, there was a gust of wind that made his favourite rocking chair rock for a few seconds. Meena somehow knew that his spirit was near her and would always be there in her need. She was glad that her boys were given so much love by her in-laws that they really didn't miss their father much. Meena realized that living in an extended family had its own benefits. Months and years flew by, and Meena started adjusting to her new life of a widow with her boys.

Almost four years had passed since the death of her Deepak. Her boys would soon be eighteen and sixteen. Time indeed was the best healer, and she was feeling much better. She could think of her life with Deepak without tears in her eyes. Deepak would always be a part of her life. However, she had been noticing that during the previous few months, she was getting a lot of unwanted attention from young businessmen who visited the office, and Meena's brother-in-law and father-in-law did not like that. They were quite broadminded people and had no objection to Meena finding a life partner again—however, dating was out of the question as that would dishonour the family. It had to be arranged by the elders as usual. They even suggested this to her parents. So, when Meena's in-laws heard of a potential match for her in Canada, they encouraged her to go to her aunt in Canada to check out the man her aunt had suggested. Her in-laws did not want her to spend the rest of her life alone, nor did they want her to dishonour the family by succumbing to temptations. When Meena heard about the proposal for her, she did not refuse, and there was good reason for it.

About six months before the proposal, Meena had been visiting her parents in Bombay; her father was ill and they had gone to Bombay for treatment. She had left her boys with her in-laws, who adored them and would take good care of them in her absence. She was travelling by the night bus. Once her luggage was put away, she settled down comfortably next to another elderly lady. She had her woollen shawl wrapped around her shoulders. She would arrive in Bombay the next morning. As she was trying to close her eyes, she felt someone behind her seat trying to touch her backside. This sort of behaviour was common In India. She suddenly got up and scolded the man behind her for his behaviour. A young man sitting alone on a seat behind also joined her in scolding the man and asked Meena to sit beside him. Meena gladly obliged, as he seemed like a gentleman.

After the initial introduction, they started talking to each other. He told her that he was a Aerospace Engineer working in the south, and was on his holidays visiting his wife and son in Bombay.

"How come you are travelling from Gujarat?"

"I had a meeting in Surat."

She told him about her life and he about his. She asked him about the work he was doing and was fascinated by what she heard. He explained to her many things about the space shuttle and the firmament with all its heavenly bodies. He was one of the engineers responsible for the working of the engine in the space shuttle and much more. She listened to all of it with interest. Meena was always fascinated by intelligence and education. Time flew by and it was almost midnight. They were both exhausted and decided to get some sleep before the bus reached Bombay.

"Goodnight," Meena said. She turned her face to the window and closed her eyes.

All of a sudden, she felt his right hand come protectively on her waist. It was ironic that Meena, who had changed seats in order to avoid any unwanted touch, was now being touched by the same man who had wanted to protect her. More ironic was the fact that she liked it. So she sat there without a word. They were silent for awhile. Then Ravi the engineer came closer and asked her, "Should I take my hand, off?"

"Don't. I am scared because I like it too much. Any decent woman would have told you off."

"It is alright to feel the way you do. After all, you are young and have been a widow for five years."

Their faces were close now and it was dark. In the heat of the moment, they started kissing each other on the face. Never did they kiss on the lips, nor did his hand slip from her waist to any other part of her body. She was thankful to him for this gesture of decency. This alone saved her from making a complete fool of herself. Everyone on the bus was fast asleep, or so they thought. Meena could not believe the intensity of her want at that moment. It was as if all the lonely days and nights after the death of Deepak, were wanting to be compensated. Meena knew that she could not let this continue. She tore herself from him, and turned her head to the window again and tried to sleep with Ravi's hand still on her waist. By the time her stop arrived, they were both fast asleep, and were awakened by the loud announcement of the driver. Ravi quickly removed his hand, and as if nothing had happened, Meena got up from her seat and left the bus. They had exchanged phone numbers and addresses in the night.

She knew that what she felt for this man was not love. Yet, the feeling was very strong with this stranger. She knew that her carnal senses had been awakened by his simple touch. Her waist burnt with his touch for many days after the incident. Ravi started writing to her regularly after that, asking her to meet him at a place away from her house. The preposition was very tempting, but she realized that if she met him, she would not only succumb to her temptations, but also would help him do something wrong. The sense of right and wrong was too deeply instilled in her. It would have been another matter if he was single, and even then it would be a very risky venture because if caught, she would dishonour the family. She had to put a stop it. With this resolve, she wrote him one last letter, asking him to stop corresponding with her. It had no future for either of them except cause trouble and ruin lives.

This incident made her realize that she was neither immune to feelings nor to temptations. In the end she was delighted that she'd had the strength to do the right thing and survive. She was able to forget him, in time. This also gave her the wake-up call that she was fragile and, though she had been strong this time, there was no guarantee that she would be able to remain strong always. The only alternative would be to get married, she reasoned. She thought everything would be right, if she was married again.

Meena went to Canada on a holiday in June of 2001, and started dating Ramesh, whom her aunt had suggested. She would be allowed to go with Ramesh a few times before she made up her mind about marrying him. Besides, she was expected to be back at night. Meena had to abide by the

Indian rules even in Canada. She did not mind it as she knew no better.

Ramesh was a strong and tall man, nothing much to look at, except for his well-maintained body. He was very fit for his age. Ramesh was an engineer by profession. He was not only very well educated, but also from a well-to-do family. He could talk about almost anything as he was a voracious reader. Past and present politics of every country was his favourite subject. Meena could have an intelligent conversation with him during the day. However, she observed that he drank a bit more some nights. During those times, he also got angry or sometimes even cried, remembering his childhood or the betrayals he had experienced from the women in his life. He did not trust women much, but with Meena, he was good. Most of the evenings, he drank in moderation and was great to be with.

"Meena, I am glad you have come into my life. I did not trust the two most important women in my life as they were both cheaters. One was my mother and the other, my late wife. One night when I was only eleven years old and had a very bad earache, I went to my mother only to find her in bed with another man. My father was away on business at that time. It was the most devastating sight I ever saw in my life. My late wife also cheated on me with her old boyfriend who came to visit us in our home. I saw them dancing very close one evening. The next day, my wife had taken a day off without my knowledge and I found them in a hotel room. That was the first time I hit her black and blue."

Meena had no proof that all these things really happened or if they were a figment of his imagination uttered in drunken stupor—but when he narrated these events, anyone could see the hurt and disdain in his eyes. Sometimes, when men and women get jealous, they think the worst, especially if the trust is lost. Maria could not tell if alcohol had clouded his mind and judgement.

"Whatever truly happened, you certainly had no right to hit your wife. Love is a matter of the heart. You cannot force it on others. If one is bent upon cheating, one will find ways to do it. In fact, getting to the root of the problem might have solved it."

"Do you think I should have left her and deprive my only son of a stable home?"

"I am not telling you that you should have left your wife, but you certainly had no right to physically abuse her. It is better to part, at least temporarily, than be violent towards your spouse."

"Perhaps you are right, Meena. I was young and strong then and was not able to control my temper. As we grew older, there was much more harmony in our lives. The past was forgotten. Hope her soul is in peace now."

"I am sure it is. I am glad you resolved your problems."

"In hindsight people say that they would have acted differently, but I say that if the same circumstances present themselves without the memory of the past, we would act in the same manner. For a certain action, each person has a reaction based on their own needs and values. That is exactly what I did in my youth. As I grew older things changed and I became a better person."

Meena enjoyed talking to Ramesh and admired his frankness. He seemed to be in love with the female gender. He had a soft corner for women, and never missed a chance to compliment every female he encountered, whether she be ninety or just three. Ramesh was a man of the world. He had been with many women in his life, especially when he was a bachelor— many of whom were married women. He had told Meena everything about his affairs and how they started. These were some hot stories of lonely married women enticing an eighteen-year-old boy. Most of them asked him and other bachelors to come to their house to do some chores like painting or gardening. These young women would invariably seduce these young men into having sex with them. The young lads, who were starved for sex, were glad to oblige these ladies. He said that in that part of British Africa—where he'd worked from the age of eighteen until he came to Canada—there were no single girls from India, but there were bachelor boys who had come for work from India. For these young men, there were either the local girls or young wives who were, either newly- wed (and not happy in their marriages), or just wanting some thrill to get rid of their boredom. However, he said that he was faithful to his wife for the twenty-three years he was married to her.

Meena was appalled by these scandalous stories and realized that human beings were frail and seductive, easily succumbing to temptations of the flesh. That by no means meant that all young wives were unfaithful to their husbands at that place or in those times. He was very open, and she listened to his stories and laughed with him. He said that he wondered whose children were born to whom in that promiscuous society. As the time passed, many Indian expatriates left that continent and went to different parts of the world, including Canada, Australia, and the United States. As they scattered across the globe, they took their secrets with them, and a new life of order and propriety started to emerge in their lives.

Her future husband Ramesh wooed her with all his heart and within a few outings with him, she was asked by her aunt to make up her mind. Soon she was married according to the Hindu rites in the presence of few friends and family. Ramesh's son didn't attend the wedding, as he did not approve.

The next four months that she spent with him were heavenly. He took her everywhere. They travelled to Niagara Falls, Ottawa, and Montreal. He introduced her to different types of foods and wines, and enjoyed discussing politics and world affairs with her. In short, they enjoyed each other's company. More than anything else, he was there when she was most vulnerable and needed him the most. He had seen much, endured much, and enjoyed wealth. His experience had made him who he was. What they had was a healthy and fulfilling relationship. Ramesh was completely satisfied with her and told her that if he had to die that very minute, he would go happily, as he had his every wish and desire fulfilled in this mortal life.

Her extended family in India, in the meantime, had prepared Meena's two boys to face their future in Canada. However, the boys were not happy about it and detested the idea of their mother with another man, not to mention the disruption it would create in their lives. As all their friends were in Gujarat, they thought it was unfair and very selfish on their mother's part to uproot them from their loving and familiar surroundings and place them into the unknown for her happiness. How would they understand her struggles? After much explanation, the boys had agreed to go to Canada with her. When finally they arrived in Canada, Meena surprisingly found out that it was not what she had hoped for and dreamt of.

Meena was working in a retail store from the time she had come to Canada and, as a result, got odd days off. She had tried for clerical and accounting jobs as she was a C.A. back in India. After continuously being asked if she had Canadian experience from every prospective employer, she had abandoned all hopes of getting a job in her field of expertise. At the same time, it was utterly frustrating to work in retail after being so highly educated; furthermore, she had managed the accounting and finances of her husband's business, which had more than a hundred employees. Her cousin in the U.S. was never asked for American experience when she had applied for a job there. Meena got really upset with the stupid question, "Do you have Canadian experience?"

What on earth do these people want? How can one have Canadian experience if one is never given a chance? How can you reason with the unreasonable ones? She thought.

After evaluating her Indian degree from the Ministry of Education and finding out what she needed to do to get an accounting degree, she enrolled herself in university. Meena was a busy woman. She worked odd hours during the day, and attended university as a part-time student by night.

Her marriage, which had started like a fairy tale, had taken a turn for the worse once she arrived with her two boys. Ramesh was not the same any more. Though he knew Meena came with the whole package, once he laid his eyes on the boys, Ramesh changed. He wanted Meena minus the boys. He found the boys to be an obstruction and a burden. He had hidden his alcohol problem from her during her previous stay in Canada when she had come to meet him—or perhaps Meena had turned a blind eye to it. His problem was that once he started drinking, he did not know when to stop. It was surprising how he managed to go to the office every day and function so well.

She remembered how he had pampered her during those first four months. She was like his little princess. As he was big compared to her and many years older, people often mistook them for father and daughter. She had chosen to marry him because at that time in her life it was hard for her to live as a widow, and it was hard to find a respectable man who was single and willing to take on, two children. When she found Ramesh, who was so attentive to her, it was hard to refuse.

There was constant friction between Meena and Ramesh because of her boys. They were now eighteen and sixteen. The older boy was well-behaved and studious. He stayed away from his stepfather and avoided his wrath. On the contrary, the younger son, who was used to so much love by his uncle, aunt, and grandparents in the extended family in which they had lived, felt completely lost. He was quiet and withdrawn, and sometimes seemed even rebellious. He looked to his mother for support when the stepfather got angry with him for little things. The more he revolted, angrier Ramesh got. He was almost jealous of her sons and her love for them. His drinking was going from bad to worse. Everything she did for her boys irritated and aggravated him. The Ramesh she knew was disappearing fast.

Then there was the question of money. The money she brought from India was invested in their house. Her job fetched her, a very meagre salary which was not enough for the three of them, if she left him at that time. He told her many times that her older son was eighteen, and it was time for him to leave the house and fend for himself. He also said that when the younger one was eighteen, he too should leave the house. Meena had come from India, where the children stayed with the parents, at least till they finished their education—and in most cases, till they were married.

She begged Ramesh to extend the stay of her older son till he was twenty-one, and he somehow agreed. Meena knew what she had to do. Her children were all she really had, and she was not going to lose them for any man. She bore a lot of mental and verbal abuse from Ramesh. She knew most of it was because of his drinking and he was not ready to get help for his problem.

"My late wife lived with it—you can live with it too!" he said.

Meena was also mortified with the language he sometimes used. Neither her first husband, her in-laws, nor her parents had ever used bad language. Meena continued to live with him while she secretly planned her escape by saving every penny she could spare. She also found out the rules that bind the sponsor.

Meena was very protective of her boys. When Ramesh was sober, she told him in no uncertain terms, "If you ever hit my boys or me, I will not only leave you but go after you for support, as you are responsible for me and the kids for ten years."

Ramesh looked at her with disbelief.

"So, you already know the rules and laws of Canadian Immigration System?"

There was anger and resentment in his voice. Meena had no choice. She had to ensure the safety of her children. It was evident that Ramesh did not want to part with his money; on that basis alone, he would try his best not to physically abuse her or her boys.

"On the other hand, if you only tolerate my children till they are independent, I will continue to love and care for you till the very end."

Ramesh knew that Meena meant business when it came to her children's welfare, yet he was not ready to accept that he had a drinking problem and that he had to get the necessary help. Though he abused her and the kids verbally and emotionally, he never touched them. There were nights when he kept her awake the whole night with abusive language.

Two years had passed, and it was taking a toll on her family. The children missed India and their extended family members who gave them so much love and attention. Here, their mother was busy working odd hours and upgrading her qualifications, by attending night school. She knew that the sooner she became independent, the sooner she would be able to leave her husband. If she continued to live with Ramesh, she was sure to lose her kids. She did not want that to happen.

On the other hand, Meena knew the other Ramesh—the one who was a joy to talk to, the one who was fun to be with, and who was generous to a fault. What had happened to him? To where did he disappear? Did the presence of her two boys bring about such drastic change in him? She was also grateful to her husband for bringing her to Canada. This was a country where dreams could be realized if one was ready to work hard. Besides, her older son was flourishing academically. He was twenty now and was taking life sciences at McMaster University with an intention of becoming a doctor, as he had the inclination and brains for it. Though she did not have the money for his education, she knew the OSAP in her province and help from her in-laws would help finance his education; eventually he would be able to repay it all. Her younger son was also becoming more mature and independent. He had started applying himself seriously to his studies with the guidance of his older brother.

It was Monday, Meena's day off. It was the day she was going to meet her two friends at Red Lobster. Meena looked out the window of her house. She could not believe it was the same Canada of few months earlier. How drastically the seasons changed the landscape in Canada! It was like a white-clad old widow transforming herself into a young bride with her brightly-coloured sari and jewellery, studded with precious stones. The transformation from the bare trees to the budding of leaves and blossoming of the flowers was both swift and radical. Even after two years in Canada, Meena found the change of scenery nothing short of a miracle. In spite of her situation at home, Meena was glad to be in Canada, and these friends were an added blessing. Meena was excited to meet her friends. She dressed with great care and left the house.

Chapter 3
ANNA

Anna had a unique history of her own; her mother was one of the Polish kids who had travelled from Siberia to India after the war. Their journey had taken them to India through Iran. Before 1947, India was a cluster of kingdoms. The British had managed to annex many of the kingdoms through unfair laws; one of them stated that if a king had no natural heir to the throne, he was not able to pass on his kingdom to anyone else. In that case, the kingdom was annexed by the British and became a part of the British Empire.

The Polish women and children who had come to India landed in one of the kingdoms with a king. This Indian king is said to have given them shelter in his kingdom. Though Anna did not remember the name of the king or the kingdom, she clearly remembered her mother say that the king of the land was good to the Polish people. They had plenty of food, unlike in Siberia, where they had almost starved to death. Her mother, who was only a teenager then, had nothing but praise for the king and his generosity. She had remembered her mother saying that there was a particular young man she liked, or perhaps more than liked, in that mysterious land.

Anna's mother had recalled with great tenderness the name of this young man: Pankaj. Anna remembered her mother talking about him one day, out of the blue. They had been walking in Quebec by the river Laurence, on one of their holidays, after the death of Anna's dad. All of a sudden, Anna's mother clutched her hand and said, "It was by the river that I had met Pankaj."

"Who?" Anna asked.

"Oh! He was the young man I met during our stay in India. He was so handsome, polite, and respectful. I still remember the day I met him. My two friends and I were wading in the river, and there came this handsome young man with his straight brownish hair and wheat-coloured skin, gesturing for us to get out of the water. We just stood there and stared at him, not knowing why we were not allowed to walk in this beautiful river. He then got down from his horse and literally guided us out of the water. His eyes were glued to mine and mine to his. He had the purest eyes I have ever seen, and they were filled with admiration and an emotion that I could not pinpoint at that time. Something had churned in my heart, then. When we were on our way to our camp, he waved at us and gave that most dazzling smile of his and rode away. It was only later that we came to know that he was the soldier assigned to our welfare; the river we were wading in, had dangerous currents that had claimed the lives of many. Pankaj came every day to our campsite, met the elders in our group, and provided us with food and whatever we needed. Every time he came, I knew his eyes searched for me. Only when he had seen me—and once I had smiled at him—did he leave our camp. If only our eyes could speak!

"Pankaj was our guardian, but he was so proper in his behaviour that I knew he would never cross the line and do anything improper. We both knew what the other dreamt and longed for, and what the reality allowed us, yet I waited for his arrival each day, and I am sure he could not wait for his visit, either. When our eyes met for few brief seconds, we said volumes. It was then that I wished he was one of us or that I was one of them. I was very young and so was he.

"When finally our day of departure arrived, he came to me and took my hand. After touching it to both his eyes, he kissed it tenderly and held on to it. That was the only physical contact we ever had. His eyes were filled with love and tears. My heart was overflowing with so much emotion and warmth that tears just flowed from my eyes and wet his hands. I knew then that what we had was the purest and the most selfless love there could ever be. I also knew that I would never forget him as long as I lived. Whenever I am at the bank of a river, stream, or sea, I can see my Pankaj, gracefully striding towards me on his horse."

"After all these years, you still remember him, Mom? It must have been love."

"Yes. It was. I am sure of it. It was a different kind of love; sweet and beautiful, almost angelic. God only knows what happened to Pankaj. I wonder if he ever thought of me after we left."

"I am sure he thought of you many times in his life. Some things are never meant to be, but that doesn't mean that they are insignificant. By the way, did you love Dad?"

"What a question, Anna! I loved your dad. He was a reality. I have been thinking of Pankaj more often since your dad passed away—just wondering where he must be and what he must be doing."

That piece of history related to her by her mother was Anna's connection to her two Indian friends, especially, Meena. Her mother and the rest of the Polish people had eventually travelled to England where she had met and married Anna's father. Anna was born in England in 1950 and her family had migrated to Canada in 1952 when she was just two years old. She was now fifty-four and looked pretty good for her age. Anna was a true romantic. Like Maria and Meena she was also a prisoner of love. It was also ironic that all three of them had lost their first husbands, whom they had loved very much. Anna's friends and colleagues were always surprised how she had lived so many years without a man in her life. It had been more than ten years!

Since the very first time Anna had heard the story from her mother about the Indian king who had given shelter to the Polish people, she wanted to know more. Through research, she found out that there was indeed a kind king in the princely state of India called Nawanagar, in Kathiawar, presently known as Gujarat. This king gave shelter to hundreds of Polish children during WWII. The name of the king was Maharaja Jamsaheb Digvijay Singh Jadeja.

The story goes that in 1942, the Polish army, along with families amounting to about 37,000 adults and 18,000 children, crossed into Iran by ship and boat. Some of them stayed in Iran, but the majority of them moved towards Afghanistan, and finally to India. The kind-hearted king of Nawanagar opened his province to the refugees and, with help from the rulers of Patiala and Baroda—along with industrialists like Tata—money was raised to open a camp in Balachadi beside his summer palace, which took care of their needs. The elders who accompanied these children were helped in starting their own Polish school.

When Anna read this, her heart swelled with gratitude for this king; knowing that Meena was from Gujarat made her very special in Anna's eyes.

The refugees stayed in India from 1942 to 1948; most of them then headed to Africa, and very few returned to Poland. Eventually, they (including her mother) went to England. She also learnt that the survivors who returned to Poland managed to name a school in Warsaw after Maharaja Jam Saheb Digvijay Singh, and to this day they remember him with gratitude. In 1999, the Maharaja was declared the patron saint of that school. Anna was overwhelmed by this information, and she told all this to Maria and Meena. When Meena heard the story about Anna's mother and the Maharaja, she felt very emotional.

Anna did not remember much about the country of her birth. Her parents settled in "Little Poland" which was in the Parkdale district of Toronto. She went to a public school, and after high school, did two years of college. Anna remembered growing up in a house where two of the bedrooms and the basement were rented. Her parents did whatever they could to make extra money. Her father worked as a plumber and her mother worked in a bakery. As a result, they always had enough food and the best of desserts.

Anna grew up to be a beautiful young lady. She had her mother's features and her father's complexion. Anna had married young to the first man she had fallen in love with. He was from the same hometown in Poland where her father came from. They had met in Canada. He was a distant relative of hers. She still remembered the day he first visited her house. She had instantly fallen in love with him. Her mother had told her that her aunt had phoned to tell her that one of these days Adam would be visiting them.

One early summer day, Anna was lying on her couch, reading a magazine; her father was at work, her mother had gone to the grocery store, and her brother Marcin was out playing street hockey with his friends. The door was open, and Adam came in.

"Hi, I am Adam"

Anna greeted him without even looking at him properly; she asked him to have a seat and continued to read.

"Mom will be back soon," she said.

He sat on the chair next to her and tried to engage in pleasant conversation. All of a sudden, she looked up and saw this handsome blonde guy with the most piercing blue eyes. She was amazed to see him stare at her with such open admiration. She was smitten by this young man's looks. They talked for a few minutes. It felt natural and easy to carry on a conversation with Adam. She saw the flicker in his eyes and knew that he too was smitten by her.

"Adam, come and lie beside me," Anna said impulsively.

Adam was quite taken aback by this request, but he was not going to deny the invitation. He did as he was told. Adam was only twenty-two and she was twenty. Anna, for all her good looks, had never fallen in love before. Thinking back, she could still remember how her heart pounded with excitement when she felt their sides touch on the couch. They lay in silence without a word or movement. They were so close that they could hear each other's heartbeats. Time stood still for both of them. They felt a very strong attraction for each other. They were in a different world and wanted this moment to last forever. They were in a daze of pure bliss.

Suddenly, they were awakened to the world by the loud voice of her mother asking her brother to come and help her with the groceries. Both got up instantly and sat on the couch quite far from each other. Anna's mother was glad to see Adam. She could hardly recognize him as he had grown so tall and handsome, since she had last seen him as a little boy in England. A flashing thought did come to her mind at that very moment that Anna and Adam would really make a nice pair. After the initial greetings and enquiries about family members, they started talking about Adam's plans for the future. Adam told Anna's mother that he was planning to start his own electrical business. He had worked as an apprentice for a very good and competent man for four years, and now he felt he was ready to go out on his own. Anna's mother liked his ambitious plan.

After that day, Adam was a regular visitor to her house. Anna could not wait to see him every evening. She rode on his bicycle and they circled the neighbourhood. There were no rules about helmets or two people riding on a bicycle in those days; this was a Polish neighbourhood in the sixties. The neighbours started gossiping when they saw the two of them on the bicycle. They stole kisses and little intimacies whenever they got a chance. One day, Adam rode her to a secluded place and asked her, "Anna, do you see the women in your neighbourhood staring at us and whispering?"

"Yes. I do. My mother is quite worried about it."

"We can stop their gossip by doing only one thing," he said. Then, Adam knelt down and asked Anna to marry him.

Anna was quite shocked. He had given no hint of his intentions. Nonetheless, she was delighted. She was very much in love with Adam, and he was in love with her. Being a good Catholic gentleman, he did not want to cross the line with Anna till they got married. Anna was glad that he respected her, though many times she had wished for more.

Anna looked at him and said, "Yes. Yes!"

"One 'Yes' is enough, my love," he joked.

Adam then took her in his arms and kissed her in a manner that was different from his previous kisses. Then he rode her home and asked Anna's parents for her hand in marriage. Anna's parents gladly agreed as this would silence the wagging tongues of her neighbours. They had a small wedding, a month later.

Anna and Adam decided to live in her parents' basement and pay them a small amount for rent and save money for their house; they did not care how small or humble their dwelling was, as they were very much in love and nothing mattered. Adam got along well with Anna's parents and they were glad to have Adam who looked after all their electrical problems. Their love and attraction for each other was so great that no hardship was a problem, and they sacrificed all their luxuries to save money for their own place. Within two years they had enough money for a down payment to buy a small house on Roncesvalles Avenue in Toronto. It was an exciting time for the young couple. They started working hard to furnish their place. Everything was the fruit of their labour of love.

Within another year, Anna was expecting their first child, and Adam was delighted to hear this news.

"Oh, my sweetheart! I am thrilled beyond words. Come here." He then lifted her up, swung her around and, planting an affectionate kiss on her cheek, set her down.

"Take care of yourself, Anna. This evening, let us go to your parents and tell them the good news. Your mother will know what you should and should not do, and what you need to eat to keep yourself and the baby healthy and safe. I love you and thank you."

He ran out the door whistling with joy. He had to work harder as the baby was coming. Adam was very excited at the prospect of becoming a father, and he was going to phone his parents and tell all his friends about it.

Anna worked in an accounting firm, as an accounts payable clerk. She liked the job and the people she worked with. She was happy both at work and at home. Adam always cared for her happiness and tried to please her in all ways, unlike some men she had heard of from her friends, who only thought of themselves and their pleasure. They had a good marriage. She bore him three beautiful children, who were their bundles of joy. Adam was a good husband and provider, and was a caring, hardworking and responsible man who wanted to do everything for his family. The key to his success was his diplomacy and honesty. People knew they could trust Adam to do the job well and at a reasonable cost. He built his clientele through word of mouth; greed was not a part of his strategy. Anna was proud of her husband and he was grateful for her undying love. They were basically a happy family.

Like all marriages, Anna and Adam had their share of problems. Anna was a beautiful woman with a curvy and supple body, though she was short in stature. She danced like a fairy, but Adam did not enjoy dancing—so whenever they went to a party, Anna danced with other men; when this happened, Adam got angry and jealous, and accused her of flirting with other men and not loving him. The vodka that he consumed did not help him think rationally, either.

"Anna, I saw the way you were dancing with my friend. You were too close—your body was almost glued to his. You know I hate it. You know, Anna, you looked like a bloody prostitute!"

When Anna heard this, her blood curdled. Was this her Adam? Why was he so jealous? Did he not know that she loved none other than him? She did dance a little too close to Steven, but it was because he had pulled her close. She was hurt by his words. She had already decided never to dance with Steven again. *What loser hits on his friend's wife?* She had thought.

"Come on, Adam, I have seen you hugging our neighbour Jane, way too tight. What about that?"

She had hardly finished her sentence when he charged in and slapped her across the face. Anna stood there speechless. She was devastated, hurt, and angry. Tears started rolling from her eyes as her hand went to her bruised cheek. Adam had never done this before, but she knew it would not be the last time. She went to her room and locked the door so she could think in peace. Adam flopped himself on the sofa and fell asleep, as he had been drinking too much vodka.

That night, lying on her bed, she wondered what had happened to their love. She, like most women, started blaming herself. She felt she should have apologized and not argued with him. She felt that she should perhaps ask her husband with whom she could dance. She also remembered her friend who had told her that if a man hits you once, he will hit you again, unless he goes for counselling and deals with his drinking or drug problem. Anna decided to ask him to go for counselling. Anna started pondering about the early beautiful years of their marriage and finally fell asleep.

She slept longer than usual. By the time she got up and came down for breakfast, Adam had her breakfast ready for her with a red rose beside her plate. He apologized profusely and swore never to hit her again, as all abusive men do. Anna, like most women in her shoes, was eager to forgive her husband. It was not easy for her to pack her things and leave after so many years of marriage. She had to give him the benefit of doubt. In her enthusiasm to make her marriage work, she even promised Adam that she would never dance with men not approved by him. After all, Adam was the man she loved and, if he was happy, the family would be happy and together. She felt that she was doing her part to avoid misunderstandings and fights. This was her logic and her resolve. In return he had to promise to go for counselling with her.

Adam was so touched by Anna's gesture that he was convinced she loved him and him alone, and let her dance with other men as long as he approved of them. When some of these men came on to her, she never danced with them again, even if the man was among those approved by Adam. Adam saw it all and loved her more for it. Adam also did his part and started to go for counselling for his insane jealousy and drinking problem. Things got much better after that, and peace and love reigned again in their house. As they got older, they started understanding each other better and there was greater harmony between them. Adam started trusting his wife completely to make her own decisions regarding who she wanted to dance with.

It was a pity that he died few years after they had come to such an understanding. He was only forty-six when he died of complications of the liver. His heavy drinking for many years might have been the cause of his liver disease. It was the year 1994. They had shared twenty-four years of marriage and had been happy for the most part. Anna was only forty-four at that time, but looked barely thirty. His death was very devastating and sad for Anna.

Adam had left her with a house and good savings. Two of her children were living in university campuses, and the youngest was at home. Anna continued to work in the same accounting firm and devoted her life in keeping the memory of her husband alive in her heart. It was during her husband's funeral that she had met Maria, who had moved into her neighbourhood just a few months ago. They had taken an instant liking to each other. Maria then had cooked some food and delivered it to Anna, as per her Indian custom, and Anna was grateful. Then Anna had invited her over for coffee; thus started their friendship. Maria's husband, Kerman, also liked Anna. After almost a year after Adam's death, Kerman had an idea.

"Maria, your new friend Anna is a decent lady. She is classy, beautiful, and brave. We should fix her up with my Serbian friend, Igor."

"Kerman, you are always looking out for others. I will ask Anna about it. If she agrees, let us set up a meeting for them."

Anna was still young, and there were a few men who would have liked to date her, but she had decided that dating was not for her at that time. She was still very much in love with her husband and did not need or want a man to complete her. She kept herself away from places and events that would lead her to meet men. When Maria approached her about Igor, she told Maria that she was not interested at the moment. She did not want to lead anyone on when she knew that she was not going to deliver the goods.

Of all the men she had met through work and through friends, only Mark—who was a chartered accountant—had attracted her attention. Besides his height and good looks, he was also a thorough gentleman. From the very moment he joined her firm, women had started swarming around him. They did not care if he was married or single. Anna admired and respected the man for his knowledge in accounting as well as his guidance. He was her boss and was always there to help her and those who needed it. Anna kept her distance, but had some pleasant conversations with him from time to time.

When Anna got her promotion and the company offered her a managerial position, she gladly accepted it, as her children were quite independent, and needed her less and less. When Mark heard about her promotion, he told her that he wanted to take her out to celebrate. This was the beginning of a friendship between them. That friendship gave Anna the benefit of male support and perspective. She could talk to him about work and more, and he always provided her with solutions. There was no tension, nor were there any expectations in this friendship. It was unique and special, which most of her colleagues could not understand nor believe.

She knew that she had a friend for life in Mark on whom she could count. It would be a lie to say that she was not attracted to him to some extent—he did sometimes make her heart skip a beat, but that is exactly where it stopped. Besides, she would have never said or done anything, to ruin such a beautiful friendship.

When her friends asked her if she was thinking of dating again, she would just say, "When the time is right and the right man comes along, I'll be ready. Till then I do not want to date."

"You are getting old, Anna."

"If I am getting old, I'll find an older man."

Anna stood firm in her resolve. Ten years went by, and Anna saw to it that she never brought herself near situations that would complicate her simple life. Her friend Maria was a real blessing. She relished those meetings and lunches with her, and for their next meeting, Meena was joining them for lunch. Women were capable of forging strong bonds with each other unlike men. She realized that this was the reason why it was easier for single women to survive and even be happy, without a man. Maria and Anna knew each other's stories; now they were getting to know about Meena. She was so deep in her thoughts, that she had paid no attention to the time. It was 11:00 a.m. already. She still had time for a quick bath before she got ready to meet her friends.

She filled the bath with perfumed oil and was about to immerse herself in the fragrant water when her glance fell on the mirror. She gave a quick look at herself. She had a good body for a fifty-four year old woman. Her breasts were medium-sized, still supple and hardly sagging. Her stomach was quite flat and her arms and thighs were still shapely and strong with hardly any cellulite. She was certainly not bad for her age. She was attractive enough, though not a beauty, and could make herself quite presentable with the right hair-style, dress, and a little makeup. Her skin was not very white, nor was it wrinkled like other white women of her age. She tanned well and easily. Perhaps she had the Mongolian blood in her. She was self-sufficient financially and capable of love that was strong and monogamous; she was grateful for what she had to offer if and when she really fell in love—but this was the first time in years she had even thought about it. She was surprised by her thoughts. She gave herself a quick scrub and stood up in the bath. She always liked to rinse her body with a shower. It was a warm day. She wore a pair of cotton pants with a well-fitting shirt and was ready within a few minutes.

Chapter 4

FIRST LUNCHEON
WITH MEENA

The three women met at Red Lobster. Meena was quite excited to meet Maria in person; it could be nothing but providence that had united these three women, so diverse yet bound by a unique piece of history. Maria was aware that Meena was in Canada because of her second marriage to Ramesh. Anna and Maria were already seated when Meena walked in. She looked very attractive with her shoulder-length straight and silky hair and her smart outfit. She was slim and tall by Indian standards. She had the most delicate features—thin lips, shapely eyebrows, a straight nose, and a great smile with perfect teeth. There was something energetic and youthful about Meena. If she was going through a crisis, no one could ever recognize it in the expression on her face. In the short communication Anna had with her, one thing was evident: Meena was a very positive person and always counted her blessings. Anna knew this because of what she had said to her when she had asked Meena how she was doing with this new country and new husband.

"Ramesh and I have our own share of challenges and trials, but he is not physically abusive. By bringing me to Canada, he has given me a chance in life which I would never have had in India. For this, I am grateful. Due to the mercies of the Paramathma (supreme soul or spirit), I am better off than many women, and my two boys are a blessing to me. A part of me will always remain indebted to Ramesh, no matter what I do or where I go."

Meena was a Hindu and believed strongly in Karma (actions), Dharma (duty) and rebirth. Hope and faith were her virtues. When Anna had told Maria about it, she too felt that Meena was a special person, and they were glad she was joining them for lunch. As Meena entered, Anna caught her eye. She was glad to find her friends already there. She came to them with a smile and an outstretched hand.

"Hello. I am Meena. You must be Maria. I am very sorry about your loss.

"Thank you."

"I can understand your sorrow, but I can assure you it will get better as time passes."

Maria was happy to know that Meena was from Gujarat. Kerman had a soft spot for the Gujaratis. In fact, Kerman had studied in a Gujarati School in Bombay, which had a big part in converting him into becoming a vegetarian at an early age of ten.

"Meena, I can speak Gujarati too. My husband was a Parsee."

"Wow! We had many Parsee friends in Gujarat. They are a noble race. They are decent, fun-loving, and charitable. They will never cheat you nor will they abandon you in your need."

"You are right about the Parsees. Now let's eat—I am starving"

"Me too. I need to order something soon. Would you like to order the usual, Maria?

"Yes, the usual it is."

Meena was a vegetarian who had tried chicken during her university years and with Ramesh. She had never eaten fish before. She was glad to see chicken on the menu of this seafood restaurant. Maria and Anna loved the platter with three kinds of shrimp on a bed of rice and steamed vegetables. They always exchanged the deep-fried shrimps for the ones barbequed or steamed. Meena ordered chicken breast with vegetables and rice. They also loved the hot biscuits the restaurant served before the food arrived. Anna and Maria ordered a glass of white wine and Meena ordered coke. They settled down comfortably. This was their day. They had lots of time to chat and catch up.

"So, Meena, how is life in Canada? By now you must have adjusted well."

"I have. I love Canada for its natural beauty and cleanliness."

"What do you miss the most, if anything?"

"You'll be surprised to know that of all things, I miss the song of the koel and the dance of the peacocks."

"Nothing can beat the song of the koel. We have them in the South, too."

"What is a koel?"

"Koels are birds found in all parts of India. Koels are mentioned even in the holy books of the Hindus. They are elusive birds—one can rarely catch a glimpse of them. Besides, they lay their eggs in a crow's nest. I don't know if this is because they are cunning or plain lazy. The song of the Koel is by far the most beautiful song. Peacocks, on the other hand, are not found in South India. I have only seen the peacock dance once, in the zoo in Mysore. In Gujarat, where Meena comes from, they are a common sight."

"The peacock's mating dance is as beautiful and erotic as the mating songs of the koels."

"You have to tell me more about these two birds, guys. I am completely in the dark."

Meena then told her about the mating songs of the koels and the mating dance of the peacock, when it transforms its long tail into a fan just behind its turquoise neck, exhibiting all its rich colours, while dancing in rapture, to entice the female.

"Though the male bird dances with passion and energy, one cannot ignore the pride and vanity of this bird. The saying, 'as vain as a peacock,' is truly befitting. The koel, on the other hand is nothing to look at, yet can melt a heart of stone and awaken a love long forgotten, by its song."

"Someday I would like to come to India, and witness all this first-hand."

"You shall, Anna. In the meantime, you should do a search on Google to hear the song of the koel."

"That's a wonderful idea."

"By the way, how is your friend Mark?"

"He is fine."

"Who is Mark? Is he your boyfriend, Anna?"

"No, Meena. He is a very good friend."

"In India he would be considered as your *Rakhi* brother," Meena said.

"What is a Rakhi brother?"

"A Rakhi brother is a good friend of the opposite sex. A woman ties a Rakhi—a special thread—on his wrist, and lets him know that their friendship will always be platonic, like brother and sister. On 'Rakhi' or 'Raksha Bandhan' day, girls tie this thread on the wrist of their biological brothers. The brothers in turn promise to take care and protect their sisters, for all their lives. Once the Rakhi is tied on the wrist of a friend, the relationship becomes almost sacred and the sanctity of this relationship is honoured ninety-nine percent of the time. Husbands will treat this man as the brother of his wife, and children will call him 'mama' or maternal uncle."

Anna was quite amazed and intrigued by the rich and dynamic culture of India.

In India, a woman is almost forced to make a male friend her Rakhi brother, if she wants the friendship to continue and be socially accepted.

"You are absolutely right, Maria."

Though Meena wanted to talk about her life with Ramesh to her friends, she kept her mouth shut. Maria had lost her husband recently. She remembered how hard it was for her when her husband had passed away. The conversation, therefore, went to Maria.

"How are you coping with your loss, Maria?

"I am still grieving. I don't think I will ever forget Kerman. He was my special love, a man who opened my eyes to other religions and philosophies of the world. He was the one who taught me that there are many ways to attain salvation or reach God. He strongly opposed the concept of conversion as it propagated the idea that the converter has the monopoly on salvation. I thank him for that. He called us Catholics 'frogs in the well' who have not seen nor wish to see the outside world, while believing that their well is the only—and the best—world in which to live."

"I like that analogy of 'frogs in the well,' Maria. Being a Catholic, I can easily relate to this. We Catholics, no matter where we come from, believe that ours is the true religion. I remember you telling me that Kerman was a Zoroastrian. I really have no knowledge of it."

"It is a very old religion. There is even a debate as to whether their monotheistic religion precedes Judaism. It is a beautiful religion. I got a full glimpse of it when I lived in the Bagh, with the Parsees, which is what the Zoroastrians are called in India. I lived with them for more than fifteen years before coming to Canada."

Anna had never heard of Zoroastrianism. She did not have the slightest clue about this ancient religion. Meena, on the other hand, had known many Parsees and seen their fire temples in Gujarat, because that is the place in India where they had arrived by ship. Their temples were called the Agyaries and Atash Behrams. Meena knew this because the oldest Atash Behram (which means "the Victory of Fire") was in Udvada—Gujarat. Built in 1742, it was called Iranshah Atash Behram and was a place of pilgrimage for Zoroastrians around the world. She also knew about the "Tower of Silence," where they disposed the bodies of their dead.

Maria would gladly tell Anna more about this great religion, as it would help her relive her life with Kerman and his extended family with whom she spent many years. However, she was not in the mood for it at that moment.

"It will take a long time to capture the true essence of this religion. I still remember walking hand in hand towards the 'Tower of Silence' in Bombay, and Kerman telling me that it was the place where his dead body would be finally taken. I was just beginning life with him and did not want to hear about death. I had heard about the 'Tower of Silence' before, from my friends in the women's hostel. I found the courage to tell him that I thought it was the most barbarous custom to let the vultures rip the flesh from the dead bodies."

"How did Kerman respond?"

"Oh, Anna! It broke his heart to hear me say that. He stopped walking and looked into my eyes."

Maria remembered his words: "You have not grasped the philosophy behind this custom, Maria. We Zoroastrians practice this way of disposing of our dead bodies, because we want to be useful even after death."

"I liked his answer. We continued to hold hands and walked in silence."

"In spite of all the years of friendship, you have never told me about your love story with Kerman. Talking about it might ease your pain, Maria."

Maria liked this idea.

"Let me start from the beginning. Christmas was celebrated with great pomp in Bombay. There were dances in many places and girls went with their boyfriends. Unlike Mangalore, Bombay was a free city. Girls and boys of different religions and castes mixed freely, especially if they lived away from home and their parents. Even the nuns were lenient on Christmas Day and New Year's Eve. We were allowed to come back after the dance was over, which was about 1:00 a.m. Since I did not know how to dance, my friend Leena and I decided to join a dancing school.

"I went to Bombay, mainly for adventure. I also did not believe in arranged marriages. I wanted to feel the thrill and experience of falling in love. When marriage proposals started pouring in during my last year of university, I thought that the only way I was going to escape being pressured into accepting one, was to get away from my small town. I had been reading the novels by Denise Robins and wanted to fall in love with a tall and handsome man. There were only limited authors that were available in our library as our college was Catholic. Most of the professors were nuns. There was little chance that I was going to find someone in South India who was more than five feet nine inches tall. Bombay was another story; there were people from the North who were tall. With this in mind, I had gone to Bombay and then to the dancing school.

"The dancing school in which my friend and I were enrolled had only female teachers who taught the foxtrot, waltz, twist and shake (which was the modern dance of that day). We attended the classes regularly. On weekends, however, the men joined the group so that the ladies could practice. It was there that I met a tall and handsome man who looked very classy. He was over six feet tall and very light-skinned for an Indian. When I saw him I remembered the heroes in the novels. I saw him staring at me from the very beginning of the practice class. Within fifteen minutes, he was my dancing partner. We danced the waltz, with him turning and swirling me around. My heart started beating a little faster every time our bodies brushed against each other.

"Who was this man? I was curious to know. By the end of the class he told me that he was a Parsee and his name was Kerman. They were called the Parsees because the first batch of them came from Paras, a place in Persia. He also told me that all dancing schools in Bombay had a bad reputation and decent women did not come to these. When I asked him why he was there, he said that he was expecting his visa to Canada or the U.S. and therefore wanted to learn ballroom dancing. By then I was quite proficient in Foxtrot, Waltz, and the Twist. Besides, I had started liking this handsome man and wanted to please him. So, I agreed not to go to these practice classes. It is then that he explained to me that most of the men who came on weekends were there to pick up girls for not so honourable a purpose, and offered to drop my friend and I back to the women's hostel. He asked me if he could see me at 6:00 p.m. the next day. I declined his request politely."

"Why didn't you agree to go out with Kerman?"

"I was very reluctant to go out with him because he was of a different religion, and I did not know him well enough. As much as I was attracted to this young man, I knew it was going to be a very complicated affair. I did not know if I had the stomach for it. He, on the other hand, knew what he wanted, and continued to phone me at the hostel. We talked practically every day. After about two months, I invited him to come to the parlour of the hostel where young men and ladies met in the presence of the nuns and talked in a respectable manner.

The couples were allowed to sit in open sight of the nuns who walked up and down. The huge parlour had many round tables with chairs. The nuns soon detected that Kerman was neither a Catholic nor Indian. When Kerman left at the required time of 7:00 p.m., the warden of the hostel came to me and asked me about my friend.

"Maria, who is your friend? He looks like a Parsee. Should I dare to say that he looks like Jesus?"

"'He is a Parsee, Sister Angelina, and his name is Kerman. We are just friends.'

"I saw the colour drain from her face. She was visibly upset. 'It all starts with being just friends. You are both young and you do not know when things might change.'"

"I really did not care for her lecture, nor did I want to argue with her. I just said, 'Thanks for the warning, Sister. I'll remember it.'

"Kerman came every day to see me at the hostel and our conversation was always about religion and vegetarianism. We discussed and argued passionately about things that mattered to us. He said that though he was born a Zoroastrian, he loved the Bhagavad Gita, the holy book of the Hindus."

Anna, as usual, wanted to know what the Bhagavad Gita was about. Maria explained that the war of Mahabaratha was fought between two brothers and their sons. Arjuna was the son of one of the brothers and Krishna was an "Avatar", or reincarnated form of one of the Gods. He drove Arjuna's chariot. Gita was the written record of the conversation between Lord Krishna and Arjuna. Arjuna was a reluctant participant of this war, because it involved the killing of his own cousins. Lord Krishna finally managed to convince Arjuna to take part in this war by telling him that it was his duty or Dharma as a Kshatriya (warrior caste) to fight, and the action or Karma could not be deemed good or bad when one was doing his duty. That is exactly how Kerman had explained it to her.

However, Maria had still argued that Arjuna was right in not wanting to kill his cousins for the sake of property. She told Anna that Kerman could not be silenced. He further argued that when the body was destroyed the soul lived on, and took another Avatar or form depending on a person's Karma in this life. Arjuna was told by Krishna that since the body was like a garment, and that when one was destroyed a soul could wear another, Arjuna should not be worried about killing the temporary body, as his immortal soul would continue to live on. Man, Krishna said, goes on coming to this earth in different forms till at last his soul or Athman joins with the universal or great soul, the Paramathman. Arjuna should therefore concentrate on his Dharma (duty). That was how Krishna was able to convince Arjuna to fight.

"That is the most uncomplicated way of describing the teachings of the Gita!" Meena observed.

"That is how Kerman was. He made complicated things simple. We were two different people, brought up with two entirely different set of values and beliefs—yet there was a very forceful attraction between us. We argued intelligently and passionately, admiring each other's convictions and rationalization of them. I admired his open mind, his acceptance of other religions and the ability to see below the surface to find good in each of them. Kerman told me that he believed in philosophy and spirituality rather than the confined, ritualistic part of any religion, including his own. I was brought up—or shall I say brainwashed—to believe that Catholicism was the only way to salvation and heaven. Considering other religions, even Protestantism, was not good enough for me, till then—so you can imagine what I thought of Kerman, initially.

"Gradually, I changed my attitude and started waiting for his visits. To add to our differences, he was also a vegetarian because he believed in non-violence, and killing for him was the greatest of all sins. According to my Catholic worldview, all nature and the creatures in it were created for the pleasure of man who was the highest form of God's creation—hence killing and eating an animal was not a sin, but rather a gift from God. Furthermore, for me and the Catholics who were hung up on nothing but sex, all sins originated and ended in sex.

"For Kerman, sex was spiritual, as long as it was between two loving and consensual human beings, used as an expression of their love for each other. It was sin only when it was purely used for the gratification of senses."

"You know, Maria, both Anna and I married our own kind. Anna married the man she loved from her own background, approved by her parents, and I fell in love with the man I married who was chosen and also approved by my parents. You are the only one who really dared to go against all norms, for love. That makes your story so special and interesting."

"It is indeed an interesting story. I, who had initially fallen for his looks, was now falling for his beautiful mind and heart. He proposed to me on the first night we went out. Our talks on the phone and in the parlour had brought us closer and helped us understand each other. Though I was surprised at the unexpected proposal, I knew in my heart that I would marry no other. Kerman said that he was twenty-eight years old, and he knew that I was the woman, whom he wanted to marry and spend the rest of his life with. He said he did not want to waste any more time. Although I knew the repercussions of accepting his proposal, I had done it anyway. It was then that he kissed me for the first time, and it was my first kiss ever. It was December, 1965."

"How long did you know him before you said, 'yes'?"

"Perhaps little more than six months, but in Indian standards and within the culture of arranged marriages, this was plenty."

Maria then told her friends that telling their parents was another major task. Maria's family was staunch Catholic, and Kerman was the only child of his loving parents, who had pinned great hopes of him marrying into an affluent Zoroastrian family. It was surely a no-win situation for both. Maria was the eldest child of five. If she married a Parsee, it would be a big scandal, and decent proposals might not come for her sisters. Furthermore, they would be devastated that Maria would go to hell. Maria had taken a bold and selfish step: she had put her happiness before the welfare of her family, and that was not perceived well in the community. On the other hand, Kerman was the only child, and if he married an outsider, it would break his parents' hearts. As it was, the Zoroastrians were a very small community in the world, and each mixed marriage dwindled or watered down their religion. They were a very proud and good people. They never converted anyone to their religion. Their famous saying was, "A Zoroastrian is born, not made." All they wanted was to preserve their ancient religion. Yet Kerman had decided to marry her, an outsider or *Parjat* as the Parsees called them.

"Kerman was waiting for his Visa to Canada or the U.S.A. He said that the minute the visa came, he would go first, and then within six months he would come back and marry me. I somehow trusted him. Before I could tell my parents, they were notified through a letter from the nuns of the hostel. I did not know of this. Therefore, when I got a telegram saying that my mother was seriously ill and that I should come home immediately, I was devastated and I ran to Kerman to show him the telegram. He had one look at the telegram and told me that it was just a ploy to get me home.

"Was Kerman right?"

"Yes, he was. My parents and my paternal uncle tried their best to persuade, coax, and even threaten me, but they failed. I stood firm. I told them that I loved Kerman, I had given my word that I would marry him, and they couldn't do anything to stop me. Even if they did stop, they would never be able to force me to marry another."

"You must have been one gutsy girl, Maria."

"My parents had placed me and my siblings in boarding schools from a very young age, out of necessity, yet that played an important role in making me independent. I was used to making my own decisions. What was thrust upon me due to circumstances had become second nature to me."

Maria then told them that the days she spent at home were not happy. Everyone was unhappy and disappointed. Her heart bled equally for her parents and her love. It was one of the hardest things she ever had to face. They could not understand how a girl from a respected family could fall in love with a non-Catholic, and then be so shameless as to tell her parents that she wanted to marry him. They asked themselves what they had done to deserve this. They were too ashamed to face their community and friends and were scared of being shunned by the society in which they lived.

It would be wrong to say that no one in Maria's extended family had fallen in love with a man or woman outside the community or religion. There were a few, but each one of them had succumbed to pressure and ended their relationships. Maria was the first one to defy this patriarchal authority and tradition. She knew that by doing this she would lose the support and sympathy of not only her family, but also the community as a whole, which is the pillar of Indian marriages and alliances. It is this support and intervention that salvages marriages when they experience problems. The community elders always intervened to bring about a compromise between couples who were experiencing problems adjusting to each other. They were able to quote their own experiences and thus support and encourage the new couples to persevere, rather than despair and give up. Maria would get none of that—however, she had no choice, as she loved this man and wanted to marry him and him alone.

Maria told her friends how one of her maternal uncles had come to her rescue. He was a man who had once loved a Hindu girl and had broken off the relationship because of family pressure to salvage the family estate which was in debt. He had sacrificed his love to do his Dharma towards his family. If he married the neighbouring planter's daughter, he would get enough money in dowry to salvage his family property. He had done just that, and in the bargain had not only received the money he needed, but also a beautiful and virtuous girl for his bride. He called Maria and told her, his story. He told her that a part of his heart was lost forever when he broke his promise to the Hindu girl. He told Maria that since she was not bound by any such problems, she should listen to her heart, and he would find a way to convince her parents. He also agreed to mail her letter to Kerman.

"He must have been your saviour."

"Yes, my friend. He was."

He had a plan. He told Maria if she wanted to marry Kerman, he would have to come and meet her family and sign an engagement contract which would specify the amount to be paid by Kerman as damages, if he broke the engagement. He told Maria that he was a stranger to them and there was no guarantee that he would marry her. If he did not marry her after the engagement, Maria may not get another proposal for marriage. At least with the damages paid, it would help Maria in her life. Maria had no choice, but to agree to bring Kerman to meet her parents.

It was then that they let Maria return to Bombay, as they were convinced that they would not be able to change her mind. She wrote to Kerman about the exact time of her arrival. When she reached Bombay, Kerman was there to meet her. She could see the joy and relief on his face. Instead of taking her to the hostel, he took her to a hotel where they stayed the night and made love for the first time in their lives. Kerman knew Maria loved him and had the courage to face her family. They were like long lost lovers reuniting. Kerman was the first and only man Maria had ever been intimate with, and that was no surprise, as most young women those days in her small town never went on dates, and always had arranged marriages. Before falling asleep, Maria gathered enough courage to tell Kerman what her uncle had suggested about signing the contract. Kerman was taken aback.

"This is our love story, not a contract."

He was angry and said he had never heard of such nonsense. Maria then explained to him the reason and logic behind it and told him that though she trusted him and was not interested in marrying another, her parents did not trust him and wanted this done for security. Kerman understood the situation and agreed to meet Maria's parents and sign the contract. Maria wanted an open church wedding, so that the honour of the family would be salvaged. Kerman agreed to that, too.

"What about his parents?"

"He never told them, as he was scared that they would stop the wedding."

"I am sure that must have bothered you."

"Sure, it did. I wanted the blessings of both sets of parents. However, they were Kerman's parents and I could not interfere. He did take me home to meet his parents as his friend."

Within a few weeks, Kerman got his visa for the U.S.A. Kerman's friend in the States had managed to get him a job and a Green Card. They were both architects, and now Kerman had a job in a reputable firm in Chicago. Kerman boarded the plane to Chicago in March of 1966. Though it broke Maria's heart, she let him go, as she trusted and loved him. Maria went back to her parents to spend the six months with them. The townspeople gossiped and looked at her with pity.

"Poor girl, her Parsee friend must have abandoned her. Who will marry her now that she is polluted? God knows what will happen to her sisters! What a promising girl—look what she has done!"

"Didn't that upset you, Maria?"

"It saddened me to learn what even some of my good friends were saying about me. I ignored it as much as I could—yet it hurt; sometimes even I wondered, *what if Kerman never returns?* Six months were like six years for me. True to his word, Kerman wrote to me every day from the States. I can still visualize the embarrassment on the face of the mailman when he delivered the open cards with love messages on them."

"Did he return on time to marry you?"

"At the end of six months, Kerman was at my doorstep to make me his wife. My joy had no bounds when I saw Kerman. He was truly a man of his word!"

Kerman and Maria were reunited again, and she knew at that moment that nothing but death would separate them. Their love was their gift and treasure. What they felt for each other was powerful and strong. Maria never considered herself beautiful, yet Kerman loved her and her alone. It was a lovely feeling. Maria did have a figure that was the envy of women and a feast to the eyes of men. Maria and Kerman married in the Catholic Church on the fifth of September, 1966, according to the wishes of Maria and her family. Kerman, though he did not believe in this, had agreed for Maria's sake. He had even agreed to bring up the children in her faith. However, everything changed when the priest who was performing their nuptials refused to let Maria and Kerman enter through the main door. Instead, he asked them to enter through the side door and sit on a bench and not on the decorated chairs reserved for the bride and bridegroom, because Kerman was a non-Catholic. Maria, Kerman, and most of the people gathered in the church were aghast at this action by the parish priest and the attitude of the Catholic Church as a whole. Kerman told Maria later that he decided not to bring up his children Catholic (if and when they arrived) at that very moment. Being Kerman, he had kept his cool and never said a word in the church or at the reception. Only when they were alone in the hotel room did he vent his anger. Maria did not blame him. All she could do was apologize and tell him that she herself had been surprised. Kerman was too much in love with Maria, and when he saw the tears in her eyes, he understood that she was telling the truth. All his anger melted, and he took her in his arms and all was forgotten. Soon, they were lost to the world.

Kerman's six months of loneliness and want for Maria was evident in his shivering touch and his devouring lips. Maria surrendered herself without reservation. It seemed like Kerman and Maria would never be satisfied of their thirst for each other.

Their love had been able to cross the barriers of religion, race and temporary distance, face the challenges and emerge victorious. They were man and wife now. There was sanctity in their union. Everything that transpired between them from that day onwards was not only special, but Holy, to Maria. They had waited patiently, neither of them losing hope. Distance had brought their hearts closer and they had grown fonder of each other. There was so much to be said, so many promises to be made, and so many assurances to be given within such a short time.

For their honeymoon, Kerman and Maria travelled to the cities of Mysore, Belur, and Halebid. They travelled by a tour bus with tourists from India and around the world. In Mysore, the two main attractions were the Mysore Palace and the Brindavan Gardens. The Mysore Palace was one of the most beautiful structures either had ever seen.

"We saw the gold throne, the bejewelled crown, gold utensils and the dance floor which was made up of translucent tiles. The young ladies danced on this floor to entertain the royal family. We were told that some of these young women were the king's concubines."

Maria would feel Kerman squeezing her hand, or pulling her closer many times during this tour. He would sometimes whisper, "Can't wait to make love to you, Maria."

"I would smile and say, 'Didn't you have enough?'"

"After Mysore, we went to see the famous temples of Belur and Halebid. These temples, which are carved out of a soft stone, are a testimony to the highest form of art. The walls of these temples, consist of such intricate work with the depiction of so many mythological stories, that one cannot comprehend the dedication and talent of the sculptors. These temples also have the carvings of voluptuous dancers in the most erotic poses. The guide explained that when the British saw these they were scandalized as these sculptures contradicted the morals and dress code of the Victorian Era. The ten days of our honeymoon flew very quickly. Very soon it was time to go to Bombay and say goodbye to Kerman. Before leaving, Kerman held me in his arms and said with so much love in his eyes, 'You were worth every moment of waiting, Maria. I love you so much. Promise me one thing and only one thing. Please be always faithful to me and I will promise to be always faithful to you.'"

"'That I promise my love, no matter what happens.'"

"What a lovely story, Maria," said Anna. "I hope the gossiping old ladies of your town gave you some peace."

"No, Anna. After dropping him off at the Bombay International Airport, I once again returned to my mother's house to wait for my visa to the States. It was the month of September, 1965. The townspeople started gossiping again— this time it was said that I was left behind by my Parsee husband who will never take me. He just married me to get what he wanted, they said. He will surely find another in the States, they whispered. My heart cried for Kerman and I prayed for my visa to arrive soon."

"Did it arrive soon?"

"Yes. It did, within two months and I boarded the plane to Chicago to join my husband. It was December 22, 1966 when I reached the windy city of Chicago in my wedding sari and wedding jewellery as it was the custom in those days for Indian brides to arrive in their finery. Thinking about it now, I feel how impractical it was to travel in the finest silk and brocade sari and the heavy wedding jewellery on such a long flight. It was so cold and my open sandals were not appropriate for the weather."

She told her friends that they started their life in Chicago with great enthusiasm. The apartment was barely furnished as Kerman had spent all his six-month earnings on travel, wedding, and the honeymoon. Neither of them cared about the bare apartment. It was their home and they were going to build it together. They were both young and their whole lives were ahead of them. They were so much in love that there was no place in their one bedroom apartment that they did not make love. If they went out for a party, they couldn't wait to return home. The minute they were inside their place and the door was shut, they were at each other with the same urgency and want as if it was their wedding night. Kerman had eyes only for Maria, in spite of many women vying for his attention. Even some of his bachelor friends teased him that he was more in demand than they were, in spite of being married.

"That is because I am not easy to get. If I started flirting with the women, soon my demand would disappear," Kerman would reply.

It was only when Maria became pregnant that she had insisted that they let his parents know about their wedding. Kerman agreed reluctantly.

"You mean to tell us that his parents did not know about your wedding till that time?"

"Yes. I wrote them a letter apologizing for the delay in informing them and assuring them that their grandchildren would be brought up as Zoroastrians."

"What was their reaction?"

"They not only forgave us, but were overjoyed to hear about my pregnancy. They welcomed the good news with presents both for the baby and myself. Kerman was pleasantly surprised and relieved and at the same time grateful to me for writing the letter."

"How long did you live in the States?"

Maria told them that they lived in the United States for five years during which time they visited almost all the houses and buildings built by Frank Lloyd Wright, Mies Van der Rohe and Le Corbusier. Frank Lloyd Wright's, "The Falling Waters," built on a waterfall, was the most intriguing and unique house seen by Maria. The ceilings were quite low in this house and each time one entered into another room, a surprise would be waiting. By the end of the five years with Kerman, Maria was quite proficient in recognizing the architect by the look of the building. While in the States, Kerman worked for renowned architects in Chicago, Syracuse and Costa Mesa, while Maria worked wherever she could get a job. She had no trouble getting jobs in the States. All they did, was give an English and Math test. If you did well, the job was yours. It was a fair and equitable system. Maria worked for Proctor and Gamble in Chicago, Needham Harper and Steers in Costa Mesa and West Tailor Company in Syracuse. Their daughter was born in the States. They returned to India in the year 1972 to fulfill Kerman's dream of starting his own architectural firm.

By the time they returned to India, most of their American friends had been drafted in the Vietnam War and many a bride would be left alone or with very young kids. Later on, Maria came to know through correspondence that many of those marriages fell apart because of the absence of the husbands. Kerman was glad that he was not a citizen of America at that time, and therefore was not obliged to be drafted in the army. Kerman and Maria had a very good experience during their stay in the United States. Indians were treated with great respect there. Most of Kerman's Indian friends were doctors, dentists, engineers or architects and all the wives were university graduates. As a result, they all had good jobs and maintained a very good standard of living. The Americans admired the saris the women wore, practically every weekend, for an Indian movie or for Christmas and New Year's Eve dances. They were well-respected and admired, and her experience in America was indeed a positive one. New adventure was awaiting Maria in India.

It was not true that Maria and Kerman's marriage was without any problems. There were many fights as well and all of them started because of each other's possessiveness. They fought with passion and made up with equal passion, and soon all was forgotten. As the years went by, they became more understanding and less critical and doubtful of each other. Maria had come to a deeper understanding about marriage and life. She had realized that good communication and honesty was the very basis of a good marriage. Maria had come to the conclusion that both women and men go into marriage with preconceived notions as to how their partner should behave and speak. In reality, none will entirely fulfill the other's dream. This truth had helped her to face their problems, without extinguishing their love

Chapter 5

ANNA AWAKENED

It was June of 2004. Anna as usual was browsing through the internet, reading about different artists, and accidentally came across the profile of an upcoming artist, Sam, who had taken up art late in his life. She liked his profile and paintings and wanted to know more about him. He was struggling to be recognized and Anna, though not an expert on art, had some knowledge of it and could see great potential in his art. Anna had dabbled in painting during her teenage years and had won some modest recognition in her school and college days. She browsed through his paintings which were displayed on his website. She noticed that some of them expressed anger, frustration, and even a bit of violence, while others were sensual, erotic, passionate, and even pure. There were paintings of Aboriginal people who were being victimized by the whites; there were paintings of atrocities committed in the name of justice which were personified as a huge bully in his paintings. There was satire, openness, and boldness in his paintings. One thing that stood out, above all else, was the fearless and arrogant honesty of this man.

People had to observe the paintings carefully to get the right message. There was also a greater possibility that the viewers could come to the conclusion that this artist was indeed just an angry and insane man expressing his frustration. However, Anna saw the artist as a wounded victim who was crying out for justice and help. His rage, Anna assumed, was the result of what he must have gone through, even though some of the paintings showed lack of restraint and appeared very judgemental.

Anna somehow felt obliged to warn him about the impact his style of painting would have on his audience. She wanted to tell him that while his goal was a noble one, the means he was using to reach it, were too harsh at times. She wanted to convince him to compromise his style for the cause and not compromise his cause for his style. His anger, she knew had blinded him. "Anger," Anna's father used to say, "makes people blind, and what they say or do in anger comes back to haunt them later."

She eagerly reread his profile and it drew her even closer to his spirit. *This is a man,* she thought, *who could make a woman either very happy or utterly miserable.* Yet she felt drawn towards him like a magnet.

Anna took courage and emailed him, saying that she was quite fascinated by his paintings and would like to see more, and would like to know the story behind them. She told him that she particularly wanted explanation for some specific paintings. She also introduced herself briefly. She sent the email and forgot about it. There was no chance that he was going to pay any attention to her. She was not of any use or importance to him, as she was not in a position of promoting his paintings or career. She was indeed surprised to receive a reply within two days from the artist saying, "I am glad someone is showing some interest in knowing the story behind my paintings. Thank you for that, Anna. It means a lot to me. I will send you a copy of the book with pictures of my paintings and a brief description of each of the paintings. I hope that will satisfy you."

Anna thanked him and told him that she would be eagerly waiting for his book. The book arrived within a week and Anna carefully examined his work. Why was she so drawn to this person? She hardly knew anything about this man. She had been free of these feelings for quite some time now. Anna wanted to tell her friends what was happening to her, but she decided against it. *It is harmless*, she thought, *as long as the feelings are in my heart and I never let him know about them.*

She felt disturbed and frightened by some of his work. This man, she thought, was perhaps capable of violence on one hand, and intense love and affection on the other. The brash depiction of injustice and corruption in his work only showed how frustrated and disgusted he was. She felt consumed with the urge to hold this man in her arms and cry with him, soothing his bruised and wounded soul. She wanted to lift his spirits and understand his plight. However, there was a voice in her head telling her to slow down and drop off this correspondence before she lost control of her senses. Anna felt a shiver run up her spine when she remembered what Maria used to say: "When the time of destruction nears, people make extreme decisions."

Anna wondered if her time of destruction had neared, too. Anna dismissed the thought. No one could destroy her unless she intended to be destroyed. As long as she kept the power of the almighty within her, she would be alright. She would walk away if this relationship destroyed her peace of mind. She could not believe the intensity of affection she felt for this very artistic man, whose paintings had captured both her mind and soul and touched her spirit.

Anna was bold enough to email him about what she felt about his paintings without any reservation.

"Dear friend, I admire your artistic abilities and your artistic style. You are a talented artist. However, your purpose of exposing injustice might be completely lost not only by the way you have expressed it in your paintings, but also the short synopses at the bottom of each. Either be less harsh or eliminate the synopses. However, you are the artist and you should have the freedom of expression. You have to paint in such a way that arouses curiosity as well as anger in others, for the injustices suffered by you and other people. Sympathy and understanding cannot be forced upon, but felt and you, Sam, have the capacity to make people feel through your art, if only you approached it in the right way."

Anna felt good after sending this email. If there was one thing she was proud of, it was her honesty, even if it meant alienating her friends. If somebody liked her for who she was, then she knew that person was her real friend. She knew that any man would be either angry or quite taken aback by her observations and comments. Hence, she did not expect a reply. Anna had neither written with caution nor with the intention of gaining his favour. She had written honestly and from her heart.

Anna had known that her openness and straight talk could put men off. Even her friend Mark had told her so. Anna was indeed amazed to see his reply admiring her guts to criticize his style. Here was a man who was confident enough in what he believed and in what he was painting, to such an extent, that Anna's outbursts or comments did not faze him.

"I am once again intrigued by your response. Thank you for taking the time to go through my paintings and express your concerns. I will certainly consider your suggestions, but I'm not going to change my style of expression."

Anna had found a man as stubborn and as strong as herself, in Sam. She felt that she had found her match. Both of them were strong-willed, daring to take chances but not ready to change for the other. Thus what started as an online friendship between the two of them gradually blossomed into love. Anna could not tell at what time of the day or hour the wall she had built around her for years came crumbling down. It happened without her knowledge or consent and she knew that it was too late and too hard to rebuild it again. Whether the wall fell gradually or it came crashing down one fine day was also not clear to Anna.

But one thing was certain: Anna, who had been asleep for the past ten years, was now awake! There had been no man in her life. She had many friends and with all of them she had platonic relationships. This man, Sam, had somehow disturbed the dormant volcano that was within her. Her body, mind and soul were all touched in an extraordinary manner; she felt as though her whole body was on fire—but she was never going to let him know. If he did not feel towards her the way she felt, she would have to digest and purge the feeling out of her. That, she knew, was going to be very hard.

They soon started talking to each other on the phone and had pictures of one another. They talked for hours on end about their lives, their interests, their family and their aspirations and goals. By the end of three months, they knew quite a bit about each other. She felt that he was too honest at times. He discussed things and events in his life that did not need to be disclosed nor discussed. He talked about his many loves and disappointments. They also laughed and joked about life and events. He told her that she gave him such joy and peace that he had never experienced before, and that he felt comfortable talking to her about anything and everything.

"Thank you for listening and understanding me. You put me at ease."

"You inspire me, Sam. I, who haven't painted for almost forty years, am painting again. I am happier than I have ever been for a very long time."

"All of a sudden I have this urge to hold you in my arms and kiss you."

Anna froze when she heard these words. She could not talk. Her heart almost stopped with excitement.

"Anna, are you there? Did I say something to upset you?"

"No. I mean, I am here and not upset. I would love to be held by you, Sam."

"I think I am in love with you, Anna. I can't wait to talk to you, can't wait to hear your voice every day, and can't wait to meet you someday soon."

Anna felt so elated by his revelation that all she could say was, "Me too."

They started talking more often. In between their silly chatter, there would be silence when one would just say, "I love you." There would be silence again and the other would whisper the same. They continued to talk more than three times a day, and by that time, they knew practically everything about each other. He "played on the strings of the musical instrument of her soul that was laying idle in its case." She felt her spirit soar high up to the heavens when she thought of him, her heart become filled with sweet affection, her mind created poetry that she never thought she was capable of. Anna was frightened, amazed and joyful with what was happening to her. He was living in Manitoba, many miles away from her. Anna wondered if it was feasible to maintain this long-distance relationship once started. Once Sam had asked, "Anna, will you relocate for me?"

"I don't think I can do that, Sam. My job, family and my aging mother are all here. Besides, it is too early in our relationship to talk about these things. Let's see where it takes us and then work out the details."

Anna knew that she would never leave her three children, grandchildren, and moreover, her aging mother. He too was unable to relocate as his work and friends were in Manitoba. *We will have to cross the bridge when we get to it,* thought Anna. She also knew through psychology that for relationships to flourish there should be two important ingredients: similarity and proximity. There were similar in most of their thinking and views, but not all. Anna knew that some of the things they differed on might create misunderstandings. Proximity could also pose another hurdle for them. The only good thing was that they were not so young and could live apart for a few months at a time, till things could be worked out between them, if that was what they wanted. Anna knew that if their love was patient and true, they would find a way to be closer to each other. Anna did not know what the future held for the two of them, but she was grateful to him for making her feel so precious and lovable. Love was not something that can be directed, at will, at a person with the least complications. Theirs was going to be a complicated affair, not only because of the distance between them but also because of some of his views on what was kosher and what was not in a serious relationship.

Anna had fallen so deeply in love, and wanted her man so much that she was not ready to think or analyze the consequences or future of their relationship. As 'love is blind,' it had clouded her vision and she was unable to see things clearly. One day, as they were talking, Sam asked her, "Anna, I wonder if it is fair to either of us to start a relationship, knowing that we are going to be apart—yet I know I have to see you."

"You are right, Sam. Perhaps we should leave it at what it is, and continue to be just friends."

"No, my dear, that won't be possible, now as we have confessed our love for each other. We have to wait and see where it leads us. It has to run its course."

Anna knew she could not be just friends with Sam. "Let's hope for the best, while preparing for the worst," she said.

"That's not positive, Anna. You will not give your all if deep in your heart you're preparing for the worst."

"You're right, my love. Let us plunge into it without any doubt. Whatever happens, I am ready to accept it."

Whatever happens, it won't be the end of the world, thought Anna. She and Sam had found this love and they were going to proceed with nothing but love in their hearts. They had to try and give it their all and had to be ready to part amicably if it did not work. It was not going to be easy for Anna to slip out of Sam's life as quietly as she had gone in. She also knew that nothing was going to destroy her. Her faith in the Black Madonna would help her get through anything in life.

Her mother had once told her that the painting of the Black Madonna had reached Czestochowa in the year 1382, and for more than 600 years the Polish people had prayed to this "Black Madonna of Czestochowa". She would surrender their love to her Madonna as she knew that what she felt for Sam was more than physical—therefore, she would not be able to forget him easily nor start another relationship. She was not looking for security or money. Her late husband, Adam, had seen to it that she was financially comfortable. She did not need any financial help from Sam. All she needed was commitment, faithfulness and, above all, love.

Anna implored to God, the fountain of all love, to help them and bless them. She also asked the Almighty Spirit to give her the strength to do the right thing. After that, she felt less frightened and more hopeful. Anna was afraid of only one thing: destroying the beautiful friendship they had by being intimate. She knew that intimacy always changed the dynamics of a relationship; people started becoming jealous and possessive and started hurting each other. On the other hand, not seeing him at all would kill her. She did not know who to tell and what to do. Maria was mourning and Meena had told her about her problems with Ramesh. She concluded that neither of them was in a position to offer her any help.

The only person she could think of was her elderly neighbour, who was like her mother. She called her and told her that she wanted to discuss something with her. Mrs. Smith was wise and loving, and above all, the least judgemental person she knew. Anna wanted to talk to her and pour her heart out. She would certainly understand her plight. This love thing was driving her crazy. She met Mrs. Smith for lunch and told her the story, her doubts and her problems. She listened patiently as she had done when Adam died. If she was disgusted or felt like laughing at her folly at this age, she did not show it. She just said, "As much as you love him, I am not sure it is wise to start a long-distance relationship. Just be careful, my dear. From what you have told me, I feel you and Sam are not on the same page. Furthermore, I'd advise you to be prepared to get hurt. Ultimately, you have to do what your heart says. Love and physical attraction are very forceful things that cannot be stopped. You will have to follow your heart."

What a great lady Mrs. Smith was! Anna had known her for almost ten years and even though she did not see her on a regular basis, she could always count on her guidance and understanding. Though she was old, she had a mind and heart of a teenager, and that allowed her to understand and guide those who sought her advice.

Anna felt relieved after her talk with Mrs. Smith. She felt more confident and at ease. Her heart wanted to meet Sam no matter where it led. It was not possible to stop the momentum of this motion. Whatever suffering she was going to experience by going ahead with this relationship, would be less than the suffering of not seeing him at all. The moth that is attracted to the light is often burnt by it, yet it won't stop. She remembered what Maria used to say when anyone knowingly ventured into a dangerous venture.

"It's like falling in the well at night, which you have seen during the day."

Anna had not understood what it meant. Maria had explained to her that in India, there used to be empty wells, dug for water, and then abandoned. These were hazardous. Wise people never walked in the direction of these wells at night, lest they fell in them. However, the reckless ones ignored those wells and walked in that direction thinking they would avoid them, and invariably fell into them. Anna knew that Maria would consider her to be one of those reckless people and tell her that she was the one to be blamed, if her relationship with Sam proved to be disastrous.

After about four months of emails and talks, Anna and Sam decided to meet each other. On September 14, 2004, Anna boarded the plane to Winnipeg. She had never travelled to this province before—then again, she would have travelled to the ends of the earth to meet her Sam. She wondered how she had hidden this from Maria, with whom she was otherwise very open. She was sure that if she had told her friend, she would say, "Anna, please be careful. You really have no idea who this man truly is."

Anna smiled to herself. Then she became serious. *What if he is some pervert? No. He cannot be.* Nothing about him, or what she knew of him, pointed in that direction. He was never a dangerous man. He was a lover and not a fighter, a dreamer, not a realist, and a creative soul, and not a destructive one. The daring part of her brain had encouraged her to take this risk. She had felt that she should grab at every opportunity for happiness during the few good years that were left in her life. She was still deep in her thoughts when the plane landed in Winnipeg. As she only had a carry-on luggage, she was out in no time.

Sam was standing with a single rose in his hand. He looked much better than his photograph. His six-foot-one stature stood out among the few people at the gate. He spotted her and came to her with open arms and held her close for few seconds. Her heart pounded with excitement. *How is it humanly possible to feel such intense passion at this age?* Anna wondered. He led her to his car, and once they were seated, he leaned over and gave her a sweet and long kiss.

"How was your flight? I am so glad you're here. I have dreamt of holding you in my arms for months. You've touched me in a very special way, my sweetheart." He stretched out his hand to hers, and Anna just squeezed it lightly. It was a short drive to the place he lived in Glenwood, in his ancestral home. It was small and cozy. She liked the look of it and the beautiful garden. *It must have been a sight to watch during the peak of summer*, thought Anna. *He is indeed a good gardener!*

Once at his place, he kissed her as she had been never kissed before. Then he released his embrace and held her in front of him.

"Let me look at you. You are so tiny compared to me. You are beautiful, my love."

"Thank you, Sam. I love you."

"I love you too, my darling."

They did not go at each other. Instead, he brought her a drink, and they sat cuddled on the sofa, talking and laughing. It was time for sunset.

"Anna, you have to watch this. Let's sit together watching the sun disappear." He then stretched himself on the sofa, pulling her close to him so that her head rested on his chest. He intertwined his fingers into hers. Thus, they sat without a word watching the sunset. Time stood still and Anna could have sat there forever frozen in time. After the sun went down, they both got up and went for a walk. Anna loved every minute of it. Holding hands, they laughed and talked like two teenagers in love and, when they got back, it was time for supper. Sam had made reservations at a nice restaurant for a late dinner. He took her out and they dined, looking deeply into each other's eyes. Again, he stretched his hand and held hers tightly. *Age is just a number*, thought Anna. One could fall in love at any age if only one is open to it. Love and passion were not the monopoly of the young.

It was only after they got back from dinner, had their shower, and had changed into their night clothes, did he lift her off her feet and take her to his bed. He laid her down gently, kissing every part of her face. Then their lips met and heaven exploded. He was urgent and loving, yet gentle; skilled yet original; passionate, yet not lustful, in his love-making. Anna was consumed with the passion and affection she felt for this man. Exhausted, they lay in each other's arms, holding each other close long after they were spent. Anna felt whole.

They spent ten glorious days with each other. He opened up to her, sharing his innermost thoughts and secrets. They discussed politics, cultures, and above all, his experience with the aboriginal people and the injustice they suffered and continue to suffer. Anna listened and felt his pain and anger.

They visited the Fort Garry National Historic Site in Winnipeg. Anna felt she had travelled back to the 1800s and the era of fur trading when she walked through this site. They visited the Manitoba museum, which took them on a journey through the province. No wonder people called it the "Prairie Jewel." Winnipeg was a city with its own charm. It was filled with parks and rivers. Anna and Sam walked in the parks and woods, hand in hand. Sam was a struggling artist, and though made some money from art, he had to find a job to sustain. Hence, he was working at the museum. He had taken time off during Anna's visit.

"Anna, I want this to last forever. Just talking and walking with you gives me so much peace and happiness. Oh my God, Anna, I love you so much. It would be a dream-come-true, if you were home to greet me every day when I get back from work."

"If I were here every day, we would soon have misunderstandings and fights, and then we would hurt each other. Don't you think that is what will eventually happen?"

"Not necessarily, my love. If we're mature enough to know that we can agree to disagree on issues and respect each other's opinions and beliefs, life could be good and harmonious. We're older and wiser, Anna, and we should have no trouble adjusting to each other's idiosyncrasies."

"You know I cannot relocate to this part of the world, Sam. My job, my family, and above all, my ageing mother is in Toronto."

"Yes, my love, I know that. Neither can I relocate. I like to be in the prairies and, besides, I have a job here and I need the job, till my paintings start fetching me some decent amount of money."

"Let's not talk about it, darling. Let's see if we can survive this long-distance relationship."

There was no doubt in Anna's mind that they loved each other and wanted to work things out. However, their obligations, jobs, families, and so on were keeping them rooted to their places.

Anna had the most wonderful ten days of her life. Time always seems to fly faster when you are happy and in love, and the hour of parting arrived before they were ready. The night before Anna had to leave, she cried with great sadness. They fell asleep very late that night, in each other's arms. The alarm woke Anna, and she got up quietly without waking Sam up. She had a shower and got ready and made breakfast. Sam got up leisurely, came straight to Anna, and hugged her.

"I'll miss you so very much, my sweet love. The past ten days have been very special. I will always remember them. Thanks for loving me, Anna."

"These days have been equally amazing for me. You made me feel so special, beautiful, and desirable. Thanks for that. Now eat your breakfast and drop me to the airport, before the plane takes off."

"Yes ma'am."

Before getting out the door, they hugged each other for a long time in silence. Then he released her, locked the door of his house, and took her to the airport. Each of them was convinced of the love of the other and nothing else mattered. They promised to phone and email each other regularly and, with one final kiss, parted.

On the plane once again, Anna was lost in her thoughts. What did she want from Sam? The answer was simple: total commitment and faithfulness. These were the only two things she would not compromise on. She had always been a one-man woman and she wanted Sam to be like that—a one-woman man. She felt strong connection and bond between her and Sam, and there was a magic that bound them together. Sam had captured her soul before her body desired him. It was true that "Nothing can cure the soul but the senses, just as nothing can cure the senses but the soul." Thus she had cured her soul through the senses.

They emailed and talked constantly. He wanted to come to Toronto in November.

"I cannot wait to hold you in my arms again, my love. Even if I just held you in my arms, passed my fingers on your face, kissing each part of your face, I would be satisfied."

"I am equally restless to see you, sweetheart. If my body sometimes craves for you, it is because our physical union is the only way our immortal souls, encaged in our mortal bodies, can be united."

"You are a true poet, Anna, and a beautiful one at that."

"You are my muse, who inspires me to paint. Since I have known you, I have resumed my painting again."

"How great it would be if we could live together and both paint in our separate rooms and come together when we needed inspiration. On the other hand, I wonder if your presence would let me paint at all." They joked, laughed, and loved. Life was good.

Love, Anna knew, just happens and cannot be directed nor stopped at will. She was glad to have lived long enough to have experienced this love between her and Sam. She knew that this rare and most beautiful thing, which even if she lost at some point, was worth life itself. She remembered Albert Schweitzer's quote:

"Sometimes our light goes out but is blown into flame by an encounter with another human being. Each of us owes the deepest thanks to those who have rekindled this...light."

Sam was the man to whom she would be eternally grateful, no matter what happened to their relationship, for rekindling her light.

Maria, Anna knew, would not be convinced that it was a good thing that Anna had lost herself so completely to this man. She would want her to go easy. Maria would certainly consider this as teenage behaviour. Anna knew Maria was usually right about things. She had a sixth sense and great wisdom. Besides, it was not in Anna's nature to be reckless or blind. She was known to analyze things and be overcautious, and that is the reason she feared that her friends, especially Maria, would be very disturbed by her impulsive behaviour. *People live with each other for years*, thought Anna, *and do not know each other.* That is what Maria is sure to point out. Yet Anna felt she knew Sam.

This was the first time since she had met Maria that she had kept something from her. Anna felt guilty. *What will she say when she comes to know that I have been communicating with Sam since June?* She wondered. It was time for her friends to know. She wanted her friends not to worry but instead just be there for her when she needed their support. She felt like shouting and telling her friends, "Run your fingers through my soul. For once, just once, feel exactly what I feel, believe what I believe, perceive as I perceive; look, experience, examine and for once, just once, understand."

Deep in her heart, Anna knew that no matter how Maria reacted, she would still understand, as they were all prisoners of love, and they were best friends.

Chapter 6

VENTURING INTO
NEW PATHS

The three friends had started venturing into new paths, with determination and resolve. Each of them had important things to share with their friends and get their approval and blessing. It had been a few months since their last meeting, as both Maria and Anna had some family events to attend.

They met again at the Red Lobster. Maria was the first one to arrive. She loved good food and was always hungry when she came for lunch. This time she was going to have a lobster with chicken breast and vegetables. It was nice that she could have such a combination. Her mouth craved lobster. She remembered how she and her other teacher friend Jenny used to go to a Chinese place in the Rockwood Mall and have the two-for-one lobster dish with rice and hot and sour soup. They used to love it.

Jenny had retired early and was now living with her son. Jenny's story was very sad. She was a Serbian girl who had fallen in love with an Italian boy in the early sixties and had become pregnant. The Italian mother of the boy had forbidden her son to marry Jenny, as she could not be of good character to have had sex before marriage. Putting all the blame on the girl, she was able to convince her son to leave her, and this spineless man had left Jenny to fend for herself. This brave woman had not only carried through her pregnancy alone with only some support from her sister—she went on to deliver a baby boy, and was also able to educate him and bring him up as a worthy citizen of this great country. Now that she was old, he was keeping her in his house. Jenny's son was a lawyer and had a maid to look after his mother at home.

"God bless him. If not for this son of mine, I would be in a senior's home by now."

Maria was glad for Jenny and marvelled at her son and his good wife. She still met Jenny occasionally.

Just then, Meena and Anna arrived almost at the same time. Meena seemed thoughtful. She was determined to leave Ramesh, who was making her life unbearable. Her life was like a roller-coaster. The ups and downs were becoming too hard to bear for her and her kids. The two boys certainly did not need this, and with their mother working odd hours of the day, they were often left at the mercy of their drunken stepfather. Meena had to work odd hours just so that she could contribute her share for the expenses. With such expectations she had come to Canada! It was not the country that had let her down, but the man she trusted and married. Her friends knew she was not happy, as she had discussed her situation with them on the phone. She was going to tell them of her decision and seek their advice. Anna and Maria wanted to know the cause of Meena's thoughtful demeanour.

"What is the matter, Meena? You look very upset. Your eyes look puffy. Have you been crying?"

"We are your friends and you can tell us anything."

Meena burst out crying. She had been holding her tears till she saw her friends. Maria held her hand and Anna passed her the Kleenex. Meena sobbed quietly for a few minutes; then she straightened herself and told them that she had to leave Ramesh for her own sanity—and for the sake of her children. Meena told them that she knew it would be very difficult to leave him, as he took almost all her earnings and she was left with very little.

"I have started saving as much as I can, and as soon as I have enough money to pay the first and last month's rent, I will leave him."

She told them about all the mental and emotional abuse she and her kids were going through.

"Oh, Meena, we did not know it was so bad. I thought you were having some rough times adjusting to this new life. We are both very sorry to hear this."

"I can lend you money if you need," offered Maria

"No, thank you. I want to do it myself. I will continue to live with him as long as it takes me to accumulate the money. All I need is your support and advice."

"Does he still threaten to harm you and the kids if you ever left him?"

"No, not anymore. He is more concerned with the support I might ask him to pay. I have decided not to ask for anything except the money I brought from India."

"If he ever threatens you again, you better tell the police about it."

"I am not afraid. As the saying goes, 'barking dogs seldom bite.' I'll do what I have to do to save my children and myself. I have never given him the slightest hint that I am preparing to leave him, after he threatened me. I have learnt one thing from living with a man with a drinking problem and that is to never contradict or argue with a drunken man. That tactic alone has saved me from physical abuse so far. I will also pray and I know that the Almighty will help me. Is it not true that 'God helps those who help themselves?' The nun in my school always used to say that."

Meena was a very religious lady with great faith in God. Both Anna and Maria hoped that all would go well for Meena. They told her that they were there to help her if she needed anything. Meena looked calm and resolved. She thanked her friends for their concern and love; this was the beauty of their friendship.

They looked at Anna and noticed that she was a bit uneasy.

"What's up, Anna? You look a bit perturbed. Is everything alright?"

"Not really," said Anna. "I have something to tell you. I think I am in love."

"Wow!" said both of them.

They could not believe Anna, who had been without a man for so long, was at last in love. They wanted to know about this special person, who had captured the heart of this lady. Anna eagerly told them about her artist friend with whom she had fallen in love with all her heart.

"He soars my spirit, captures my mind, touches my soul and electrifies my body."

"Slow down, dear friend. You are madly and blindly in love. You are on a different plane. Think rationally as you always do. When did this happen? How much do you know about this man, and who is he?"

Maria did not like this Anna, who had lost complete control of her senses.

"It is a long-distance relationship that started in June and I have seen him twice."

"What is his name? What does he look like? What does he do for living? Where does he live? The questions came pouring in from both her friends. Anna got scared. Had she really analyzed all this? She had to answer their questions, nonetheless. Anna told them all that she knew about Sam. She also told them that they have been speaking on the phone for more than four months and that she had met him a couple of times.

"How on earth were you able keep this from us for such a long time? Now I know what kept you busy for the past three months."

"Please don't be angry, Maria. You were grieving, and Meena had her own share of problems. That is the only reason I didn't disclose this to you. The name of the man I am in love with is Sam. There is a lot of potential in his art. Perhaps he will be rich and famous someday."

"He will not need you at that time, my dear. He will find women younger and prettier. When people, especially men, become famous, there will be no dearth of women. How do you know he loves you? He may be just looking for some fun or security till his art becomes a hit."

Her friends were perhaps right. *He could be after me just for the security I could provide him,* she thought. There was no knowing for sure. Then Anna's mind told her to be fair. How we judge men who are looking for a bit of security! She looked at her friends.

"Don't women look for security all the time? Meena, would you have married Ramesh if he was struggling, especially being a widow with two children? What we can afford to do when we are young, we cannot when we are older. Yes, I am better off financially than him. However, he is a proud man and would never be dependent on me. He would do any work to contribute his share. I respect him for it. Damn it, I love this guy very much. You know what, my friends; I am going to take a chance. The worst that can happen is that he may hurt me. We have all borne hurts and it hasn't killed us yet. All I wanted was your support, but if you don't give it, I'll walk alone. I came to you for understanding and acceptance and not for permission."

The two friends looked at each other. Maria felt a bit hurt with Anna's attitude, but she didn't dwell on it. After all, she was in love. They were skeptical and frightened for Anna.

"We truly love you, Anna. We will support you whatever you decide to do. A long-distance relationship is dangerous. At this age, we want companionship and proximity; something simple and uncomplicated. Please, Anna, think things through," they warned.

Anna was aware that her friends really cared for her wellbeing and happiness. On the other hand, she had experienced something very beautiful and she was not letting it slip away. Why was everyone so afraid for her? Sam was a good man and she felt happy, comfortable, and at peace with him. She had always risen up from her falls and walked with greater strength and resolve, and she would do it again if needed. She was glad her friends understood.

Maria had always been a dreamer. She was also blessed with a memory that could recall situations and events that occurred years ago with great accuracy and clarity. That was her unique gift inherited from her father. Besides, Maria loved imagining stories of true and lasting love. The thought of writing a book had crossed her mind, many years ago. She remembered joking with Kerman that she would like to be a writer someday. Though he always encouraged her, she neither had the discipline nor the perseverance at that time. But now that her Kerman was no more, she thought this project would keep her busy. Maria wanted to run this idea by her two trusted friends.

"How are you doing, Maria?"

"I have an idea and I want your take on it."

"What sort of idea?"

"I want to write a book."

"What sort of book, Maria?"

"It will be a book of fiction, with historical facts. Real life and imaginary stories will be all intricately interwoven, into the lives of fictitious characters. I also want to write about the Zoroastrian migration to India and introduce their beautiful religion to the world. I know so many real stories of great struggles and trials and many that ended triumphantly. I want to write about them and the power, magic and victory of love. I think that would give beauty and authenticity to my work."

"I like the idea. If you write the way you narrate your stories, it would not be a boring book."

"Thank you, Anna."

"It will also keep you occupied and focussed and help you deal with your loss."

"You are right, guys. Thanks once again."

All three women had chosen their paths. Meena had resolved to leave Ramesh and was working hard to achieve her goal, Anna was ready to take the next step in her love for Sam, and Maria wanted to start writing, which was her dream. This luncheon meeting had been very fruitful. All three women had disclosed their secrets and ventures and received the necessary support and advice from the ones they trusted and loved. They parted with their hearts lighter and their resolve stronger.

On the way home, Anna thought about Sam. She felt that she was still a lovesick bird. She treasured her relationship with Sam. She felt like a bird which was out of the cage and she was going enjoy this freedom by flying to every place she desired, no matter what the warnings or what the consequences.

Whenever she felt doubtful or sad, she took her canvas and painted. Painting gave her solace, helped her celebrate her adventures, and above all, gave her the serenity she needed. Through her creative spirit, she painted with ease and clarity. She told Sam about it and even sent him some pictures. He was encouraging and complimented her on her paintings. If it was true that "…of all the earthly music, that which reaches the farthest of heaven is the beating of a truly loving heart," then she was creating art through the music of her heartbeat that reached the God of love.

As soon as Maria reached home, she started writing her book. As she wrote, she thought about her late husband who had loved her to the point of distraction. The fun they had and the times they spent together, passed through her mind's eye. Sometimes she cried, and other times she remembered the good times and smiled. Memories started to come rushing like the sea waves and she knew that her hand would not be able to keep up with her gushing thoughts.

They had been in Canada for seventeen years. Maria had upgraded her teaching qualifications and had worked for a reputed school board in Canada. She had retired only a year before the death of Kerman. Kerman too had managed to get a job as a draftsman. After working for years as an architect, it was a bit degrading, but Kerman had taken it in a stride for the sake of his children's future. All their three children had done well for themselves. Kerman wanted to retire the next year and they both wanted to spend their retirement years travelling and spending the winters in India, but he had died unexpectedly. She remembered what he always used to say: "Maria, just be by my side and support me, and I will take you and the family safely across the river." When he died, she felt that he had abandoned her before reaching the shore, because of the sudden way in which he had left her. All their plans had come crumbling down with Kerman's death. It is indeed true, as the saying goes, that "man proposes, but God disposes!"

She came to understand that when the time is up, each one has to go.

Meena had received encouragement and support from her friends on her resolve to leave Ramesh. She continued to save money for her escape. By the end of that year, Meena had saved $4000.00 and she started looking for a rental place. Even back in 2005, a two-bedroom apartment in the area where she was looking cost $1000.00 a month. Finally, she found a basement apartment for $950.00 and she took it. After paying the first and last month's rent she still had $2000.00 left. By the grace of God, she also got a job in the field of accounting as she had finished upgrading her qualifications. Everything seemed to fall in place for her and her two sons. She left Ramesh with a note.

"Dear Ramesh, I am leaving you because my life with you has become very traumatic. You are neither willing to seek help for your drinking problems nor are you ready to see a family psychologist or counsellor. My children are all I have and I was not aware that you wanted me minus the children. I am not asking for any support from you except the money I brought from India. Good bye and good luck. My lawyer will contact you soon. Meena." That was May, 2005. All her elder son asked her was, "Will we be alright, mother?"

"Yes, son. We will. My job will be enough to pay the rent, groceries, and the necessities. You will have to work for your luxuries."

She took a long breath when she was safe in her own place. She had already called her friends to tell them the date of her move. She was now eager to meet her friends to share with them everything. It is true that she felt that she had taken herself and the kids away from danger. Yet, deep down in her heart, she remembered the Ramesh she had once known and felt sad that it had to end like this. *Now that I am not with him to take his abuse, I might be in a better place to convince him to seek help*, reasoned Meena. A relationship, no matter how short, is difficult to sever. Yet, it is better to be alone than in an abusive relationship. Meena knew she had done the right thing.

Chapter 7

TWISTS AND TURNS

Another Monday and another meeting! The friends had been busy with their lives and commitments. Much had happened in their lives since Meena entered their group. Anna was radiating with a special glow. Meena and Maria knew it was love. Meena, who was the baby of the group, had a smile of calmness and victory. She as always, was dressed very fashionably and they knew that at forty-four, she would find love again when she was ready. Maria seemed at peace with herself and was radiating with joy of a different kind. They greeted each other with warmth and affection.

"Meena, you look so good. What's your secret?" Maria asked.

"I am free at last. I am no more fearful of the nights nor for the safety of my boys. Since I have left Ramesh, I feel free and in control of my life. I am in a basement apartment now and waiting for a vacancy at the nearby apartment building. It makes such a difference. Ramesh and I have also made peace. He understands why I had to leave him and he admits that he was not prepared to have my grown children live with us. Being in Canada too long, he thinks like a Canadian. He says that he still loves me and wants to keep on seeing me. He has promised to go for counselling and he will be joining AA. What he refused to do when I was with him, he is now doing voluntarily."

"We are so glad for you, Meena. This move of yours seemed to have had the right effect on all concerned. Does he want you back in his life?"

"My friends, the answer is, yes and no. It has been a few months since we parted. He is aware that I will not live with him in the same house with my children, ever again, but I don't mind accompanying him to the AA meetings and counselling sessions."

"That sounds reasonable and wise."

"If my presence helps him to persevere in his resolve to get help, then so be it. Since neither of us intends to go on a finding mission for another partner, I have decided to give Ramesh another chance and start dating him again, if things progress the way I expect them to. As long as neither my children nor I are subjected to his previous behaviour, I am free to do what I think is right. After all, he is still my husband, and I did take those seven steps and three rounds with him, around the fire. Besides, for some men, it takes separation like this to realize the value of their spouse."

"As long as you know what you are doing, we are fine with it. Hope you know that we have nothing but well wishes for you."

"I know that. I also believe that if he is trying his best to make amends and change, then I have to meet him half-way. Don't you think?"

"Yes. You are a good and forgiving person."

"Though I do not condone his behaviour, I believe that alcoholism is an addiction and needs to be treated. Besides, I have got a job in an accounting firm with my upgraded qualifications and that makes me quite independent. Ramesh has returned my money and I have invested it. He is happy that I did not ask for anything more. He knows that I was not after his money."

"Are you doing this because you are scared that he will come after you and your boys?"

"No. Not anymore. He neither talks about my boys nor about deporting me to India."

"You are a brave and strong woman. He cannot deport you. You are standing on your own feet. You are neither dependent on the government nor on anyone else. Canada likes people like you. How are you managing without a car?"

"I have a colleague driving me to the office. You know, there are very kind-hearted people in Canada. I will repay her, in my own way, someday."

Anna and Maria were glad that Meena was safe and happy. Meena was grateful for this friendship. They knew that Meena's life had taken a turn for the better. She felt proud of herself. By leaving her husband, she had truly helped everyone. Besides gaining freedom and peace, she had helped Ramesh to change his path, proved to her boys that she loved them above all, and gained respect from her friends. Maria and Anna listened to her with interest.

"There is a saying that says, 'when poverty comes, love flies out the window,' but there is no quote as to what fright does to a relationship," Anna observed

"I am sure true love can find a way to work through poverty, but not fear. Fear paralyses love, and I felt it with Ramesh. Now that Ramesh is turning over a new leaf and I am not frightened of him anymore, I am looking forward to rebuilding a healthy relationship with him. I have started enjoying his phone calls telling me that I was the best thing that had happened to him in his entire life and that he misses me very much. I am also glad that I do not have to depend on him for any financial support. My job fetches me a decent pay. Being an inherently frugal Indian, and having the accounting background, I not only save a certain amount each month, but also invest it wisely."

"How are your boys, Meena?"

"My older son Ravi is living at the campus in Hamilton. He is finishing his second year of University, studying Life Sciences, and my younger one has got admission in three Canadian universities and also in the Stanford University School of Business. He wants to go to the U.S. and live with his paternal relatives in San Francisco. I speak to my in-laws on a regular basis and keep them abreast of all that is happening in our lives here in Canada. They are happy that I am able to support myself and my two boys. They are helping me with the education of Ravi, and when the time comes, they will help me with my younger son Raj's education, as well. Then, of course, there are my parents who are always ready to lend a helping hand. Money is not a problem for me, but I do not want to take money from my parents unless I have to. Ravi is already well adjusted and even likes the Canadian way of life. It is a famous saying among the Indians that if an Indian doesn't return home within the first five years, he will never return for good, no matter what he says in the beginning of his life in Canada. Raj, on the other hand, is a different kettle of fish. It would not surprise me if he went back to India in the future."

Then the conversation shifted to Anna.

"How are you, Anna? How many times have you met your man?"

"I have met him a few times, and each time, our love seems to be growing."

"Is he alright with this long-distance relationship or does he ask you to relocate?"

"Neither of us is asking the other to relocate."

"That won't work in the long run. You have to think of something, if you are serious about salvaging this."

"I don't know what to do, and I need some time to think."

"All the best, Anna."

"I feel we are compatible in all aspects and on levels. We feel we are true soul mates. We are content to be sitting next to each other holding hands or lying against each other on a couch and talking. The comfort we feel with each other is unique. We can read our own books lying close together, and then share something funny or controversial without the other getting upset or being disturbed. There is harmony and peace when we are together with no tension or pretense. When we become intimate, which we do, it is always filled with affection, passion, sensuality and desire. As a result, we find it most natural and get the greatest fulfillment in our union. We feel nothing but positive energy circling us and no human being, at this time; can tell me that our love is doomed for failure. Yet, deep in my heart I know we cannot go on flying to another province to meet each other. It is not feasible in the long run. I need to examine the situation in an objective manner and come to some conclusion, which may even mean parting from each other."

"Now I can say that the Anna I knew is back. You are being reasonable and logical."

"Facts and circumstances have pushed me to face reality of our relationship. However, it does not mean I love him less or will ever forget him. Besides, I can face anything with friends like you two."

The friends parted. Each and every meeting allowed them to unburden their hearts and open their minds. They always parted with greater confidence, determination and clarity.

There was a twist in the course of direction that both Meena and Anna were taking. Anna had decided to face the problems in her relationship with Sam head on, instead of burying her head in the sand. Sam had told her many times that it was not fair for them to be apart when they loved each other so much—and he was right. He had also said that they had only few good years left in their lives, which were being wasted, by living apart. Anna was aware of the fact that although, she could live apart from Sam for months, he couldn't. She needed to take a hard and deep look at their relationship, and come to some decision. If she couldn't be near him, it was only fair that she let him go without making him feel guilty, no matter how much it hurt her.

Meena had embarked on a journey of reconciliation with her husband, after leaving him. Meena was a woman who believed in second chances. She had given her late husband, Deepak, a second chance and now she was doing the same with Ramesh.

Maria was the only one going ahead with her dream of becoming a writer.

Chapter 8

MEMORIES

Memory is a way of holding on to the things you love, the things you are, the things you never want to lose.—Kevin Arnold

Maria's photographic memory took her back to the days when she was a child. Her very first memory was of her baby sister. It was the year 1949, and she was not quite four years old. Still, she remembered returning from the hospital in a horse-drawn carriage with her mother and her just-born sister, with great clarity. How fragile and beautiful she was, and how proud Maria was of her sister! She also remembered her chubby brother, not even two years old, kissing the baby's hand; her mother was as beautiful as always, and was sitting with the baby on her lap.

Thinking back, she realized her best memories were of the time she spent on the coffee plantation during the holidays.

Life on the plantation was heavenly compared to the city or town. Her family lived in a big bungalow with servants that tended to all their needs. Her father managed the plantation, kept the accounts, and looked after the buying and selling. Maria's father was only eighteen when he started working in the plantation at his father's request (and as a favour to his cousins). He had finished his Inter, which was two years after high school, and wanted to continue his studies. But his father's cousins, Paul and John, had started a coffee plantation and wanted some help in accounting and management, as their own children were very young.

Maria's dad was upset at first, but then adjusted to the idea, as life in the plantation was not so bad after all. He always had more than enough to eat. The work was not so hard and his uncle had also promised him part of the plantation. His future was secure and he had nothing to worry about. Maria had lived in the plantation only till she was five years old, and then afterwards only came for holidays, but it still had great impact on her life. The most beautiful memories that sprang out of her mind were connected to this innocent part of her life.

Coffee was always grown on slopes so that there would no stagnant water at the roots of the plants. These plants also needed shade to grow. Some planters grew pepper as an inter-crop, which also provided the needed shade. These planters would plant Silver Oak trees to give shade to the coffee plants. Since Silver Oak had all the branches only at the top of the tree with no leaves on the trunk, the pepper vine could easily go around it. It was a pleasure watching how the workers picked the pepper once it was ready. They would lean a bamboo ladder to the oak tree. Once it was safely placed against the tree, the men would climb and pick the pepper, and put it in the pouch tied to their waist. There would be two men for each tree to cover the vine around the trunk. They would climb as high as the vine had managed to travel, as long as the bamboo was strong enough. Once the pepper was picked, the green ones would be dried with the husk to make black pepper, while the red ones were separated from its husk to make white pepper. One could see how the pepper obtained its black colour once it was dried. Some planters even grew orange trees to give shade. Intercrops changed according to the demand for the product and cost of maintenance. Spices, such as cardamom and cinnamon, were also grown as intercrop. These aromatic spices added flavour to the coffee.

The most beautiful sight Maria remembered was the blossoming season, which she saw during her summer holidays (April-May). During this season, the coffee plant would be filled with white flowers that bloom in all their beauty. These flowers bloom on the stems of the plant, in bunches, and at certain intervals. One stem, therefore, could have as many as ten bunches of white flowers on them, depending on its length. This sight of green plants sprinkled with white flowers was simply a feast to any eye. Oh! And the scent they emanated filled the air! It was just heavenly walking through the plantation during these days, as it satisfied both the sight and the olfactory senses.

The blossoming season was usually during the months of March or April after the plants had received between one to two inches of rain. The blossoms lasted only for seven to nine days. When the flowers dropped, small green seeds appeared. The crop depended on the blossom each year, and the blossom depended on rain at the appropriate time. Maria remembered her father walking up and down, looking at the clouds and hoping it would rain. He knew exactly which clouds brought rain and which were just passing by. Those were the days, when there was no spray system. Nowadays, because of artificial rain through irrigation from the third week of February, the blossoms come early.

The picking season of Arabica coffee was equally fascinating. She had witnessed this during her Christmas break. It was a season when the fully-ripe coffee seeds were picked. These ripe coffee seeds turned reddish-purple in colour and, although they appeared to be luscious and tempting to the eye, were not edible. The coffee picked directly from the tree was supposed to be the best coffee. The beans that had already fallen were picked up later and cured separately. The coffee beans were and are picked by women, some as young as fifteen. Maria had seen strong untouchable women, bring their loads of coffee that they had picked during their day's work, to be measured in a bushel so that they could get paid according to their pick. Some of these girls and young women were dark in colour, and had the most exquisite features and bodies. Their full bosoms, strong legs, curved backs and shapely arms were visible even through their modest saris. They looked amazingly beautiful, walking erect, supporting the loads on their heads with one hand, while the other arm swung at the side with a perfect gait. This was beauty in its purity and simplicity. Some of the young men were no less in their good looks, but were seen only in the plantation doing harder work.

Maria also remembered the scandals that went on in the plantation. There were rumours about how some of the neighbouring landlords were gratifying their desires by sleeping with these young untouchable girls—virgins as well as young wives. This was not discussed openly. One could only hear it when the servants gossiped. Some said it was rape and others said that the women obliged as they were powerless to refuse the landlords, as in those days these untouchables had no protection, no unions, and as a result, no ability to defend themselves. Besides, the high-caste landlords believed that they were elevating the status of the untouchable girls by sleeping with them. *How arrogantly ignorant*, thought Maria when she had heard this from one of her friends. Maria knew these rumours must have been true, as there is 'no smoke without fire.' How sad for these young women and their husbands and fathers! She wondered how many of these plantation owners had their seeds planted in the bellies of these untouchable women.

From a very young age, Maria was aware that power corrupts all. *Power,* Maria thought, *is a strange thing. The true character of a person will be known only when he or she has power. People in power do the things they do because they can get away with it.* Maria was glad that things had been changing rapidly in India. On her last visit she had found that all untouchable families were given a plot of land to build their own houses. Basic food such as rice, wheat, lentils and a certain amount of sugar was given to them at a very nominal price. As a result, very few lived on the plantation and went to work only when they felt like it. The unions were strong and had set a daily wage that was reasonable with medical benefits, bonuses, and the clothes required for the job. The tables had now turned, and the landlords had to woo the workers with extra incentives, especially during the picking season. Maria was glad and proud of the Karnataka State where she came from. The planters were not sitting idle, either. They were encouraging the inventions of different machines that could do the job of the workers. Maria knew that it was just a matter of time before the machines took over manual labour and put these poor untouchables out of work, altogether.

When Maria was young, she remembered how the untouchables always kept their eyes down as a sign of submission, modesty, and respect while talking to her parents. She had seen how some of those who worked in the barn and the stable held their bowl for food in both hands. Once food was served in that bowl, which was made up of coconut shell, they retreated walking backwards till her mother was out of sight, as if she was the queen. Maria had asked her mother why she couldn't give them, proper plates; she was told not to ask silly questions and that it was the custom of the land. Though her mother did not talk about the caste system like her father, she was very particular in following that which was a tradition, while Maria always questioned.

When Maria was seven years old and they were going to church in a bullock cart—which would be lined, first with a soft quilt and then a sheet—she had noticed their little servant girl walking beside the cart with the men (only ladies and children sat in the cart). Maria had asked her mother why the girl could not come in the cart, as there was enough room. Her mother's reply still rang in her mind: "Shoes are worn on the feet, and the hat on the head. Don't try to wear the shoes on your head."

At that age, Maria really did not understand what her mother meant, but the tone of her voice had told her not to question any further. She had tried to make sense of it, but had failed. She knew her mother was upset, and Maria did not have the nerve to ask for the clarification of her comment. It was only years later that she had understood that she wanted to keep the servants in their place. Maria wondered if her mother was a snob or if it was simply that she did not ever question the status quo and therefore knew no better. That is what her mother had taught her and that was what she was following.

Maria wondered what Anna would think reading all these things in her book.

The plantation also provided Maria and her siblings with lots of adventure and entertainment. The greatest fun they had was going to the top of the hill where the plantation ended and the jungle started. It was exciting to climb, but was also dangerous as there were wild animals in this jungle that bordered the plantation—including tigers. She remembered how they used to be warned not to go to the top after 5:00 p.m. It was a long hike. When they reached the top, they sat on the rocks and had a picnic. The children would be between the ages of seven and fifteen. She remembered going into one of the caves and finding porcupine quills in it. They had taken them home, cleaned them, and used them as pens by dipping them in ink. Once they had even gotten lost and were found at last by the search party with no harm done. Hiking through the plantation, eating berries from the trees, drinking water from the natural springs and admiring the sheer beauty and purity of nature made those holidays worthwhile.

Her brother was an expert crab catcher. He knew exactly how to catch them and twist their claws without getting hurt. She used to follow her brother with a pot for the crabs. These were called rock crabs as they would be found hiding under the rocks. Maria wondered if their entertainment was torture to the crabs! They had taken these crabs home and asked their butler to cook them. He had laughed at them saying that it wouldn't even provide a teaspoon of flesh. From then on, they never caught those crabs, and that ended the crab torture.

The food was all homegrown on the plantation. Chickens were bred at home, and there were lots of cows and buffalos for milk. From the milk they made yogurt, butter, and ghee. Rice, vegetables, and fruits were also homegrown and plentiful. Food was good and in abundance, and the air was clean and fresh. Maria thought that if she was so healthy today, she had to give credit to their life of natural simplicity. Except for some store-bought biscuits, there was nothing they ate in those days that was not home-prepared. Even in the boarding schools she had attended, the food they ate was all homegrown and home-cooked. Her mother was an expert in making halva and toffee from all the fruits that were readily available on the plantation. Since bananas of every variety were plentiful, her mother sliced the ripe bananas, dried them, and bottled them with honey that was freshly-squeezed from the beehive. That was one of their desserts.

Another most beautiful memory was about the baby deer. Maria's father loved hunting. It was the sport that he enjoyed the most, and it also provided meat in that part of the world. Only men went hunting; the women and children stayed at home waiting for the game. Once, her father shot a deer and brought home two baby deer with the dead one, because he had found the babies after he had killed the mother. The meat was usually distributed and eaten, and the hide would be cured and displayed on the wall with the head and antlers; that was the routine. But that day something special had happened, as there were two baby deer. Her mother had refused to take a share of the meat. Maria's mother loved those babies. In the beginning, she fed them milk in a bottle. It was such a beautiful sight to see her father giving the bottle to her younger sister and her mother feeding the baby deer. Maria still had the picture taken at that time. When the babies were a little stronger, her mother had asked the servants to put them in the stable to see if the weaning cows would allow them to feed on their milk. Lo and behold! The cows let them suckle and the deer grew big and strong in no time. Soon they grew to be taller than the cows and the male grew beautiful antlers. How gracefully the two deer walked with the herd of cows! Maria wondered if we humans could show such love to our own species with a different colour. Maria remembered how majestic these two deer looked and how tame they had become.

They were as happy as one family, till one day when one of the deer did not return home with the rest of the herd. Everyone wondered what had happened to it. Perhaps it became easy prey for one of the wild animals; no one knew for sure. The deer had no clue of the predators or dangers of the jungle, as they were so very protected and domesticated. Once one of them disappeared, the other died soon after. Everyone thought it died of a broken heart.

There were things that Maria dreaded the most on this plantation, and those were the huge bees and beetles that came into the house during the night, because of the light. She was very frightened of them. She was also terrified of the insects and reptiles that sometimes crawled into the house. The blood sucker, huge spiders that looked like Black Widows, the centipedes, and the millipedes were some of the bugs she detested. She was glad that she was not in the plantation during the rainy season, as that would have meant dealing with even more bugs, insects, and bees.

The schools reopened during the rainy season and they had to go back to town. When she had visited her mother's plantation, she had also found that many planters had started something called "Home Stay." Here the guests stayed with the owner's family, and not only enjoyed the food and hospitality, but would get daily tours and hikes, experiencing life on the coffee plantation, first-hand. This was available for an exorbitant sum of money. This concept had become a great hit both with the rich Indians and foreigners who visited South India.

Her memories of living with the Zoroastrians in the 'Bagh,' in Bombay (Mumbai) were equally fascinating, but that would need another chapter in her book.

Memories are our greatest treasure and they keep us connected to the past. What a person remembers, or wants to remember, depends not only on the impact it has had on his or her life, but also on the mindset of the person. "Memory is the fragrance that lingers long after smelling the flower."

Chapter 9

THE ZOROASTRIANS

It was in Bombay, living in an extended family with the Zoroastrians, that Maria got a true glimpse of this beautiful ancient religion and their various rituals and beliefs. She had lived with the Parsees for fifteen years. Maria remembered entering the apartment in a Bagh, where her in-laws lived. The word *Bagh* translates to *garden*. A Bagh was a large apartment complex which was surrounded with high stone walls and two gates. It was, in fact, a gated community, built by the Wadias, one of the affluent Parsee families. These strong, stone buildings contained large apartments for which the Parsees paid pittance as rent, compared to the rent the rest of the people in Bombay paid for such a large place. As a result, the Zoroastrians living in a Bagh had a lot of disposable income left for luxurious items and they lived in style and comfort.

These clusters of apartments were built exclusively for the Parsee community. These gates were and are guarded by watchmen, usually from Nepal. Inside the Bagh there was a place for worship, a large playground and a clubhouse for adults to play cards or table tennis. In the clubhouse there was also a cafeteria. The playground consisted of a soccer field, a volleyball court and a cricket field. Every evening the maids went down with the little ones, children played, older ones took leisurely walks, some men played cards and some women gathered at the bottom of the stairs in each building to share the events in the community or gossip. Since there were no elevators in these buildings, many men and women became housebound once they had a major heart attack, stroke, arthritis or any other disabling disease.

It was a beautiful sight to see older couples walking with their hands intertwined at the elbows like old British couples. The younger generation was allowed to date and mix freely with the opposite sex and it was not an uncommon sight to see couples as young as fourteen and fifteen smooching under the various staircases. While being true to their religion, they were more western in their outlook on life and their dress, than the rest of the Indians.

Maria learnt that the Parsees were a patriarchal society. If a Parsee man married an outsider, she was allowed to live in the Bagh and make her children Parsees, while the girl who married an outsider was asked to leave the Bagh and couldn't bring up the children in the Zoroastrian faith. During the time Maria lived in the Bagh, there were very few outsiders, and as a result, everybody knew them.

Maria still vividly remembered the day she first stepped into the Bagh. Her mother-in-law had insisted that she enter the apartment with her right foot. Soon, her forehead was marked with a red powder; rice was placed on this wet powder; some was circled around her head three times and then thrown on her and Kerman. An egg and coconut were also circled around their heads and broken. Later on, Maria was told that all this was done for good luck. Maria also found out that most of these customs were taken from the Hindus and had nothing to do with the Zoroastrian religion.

"Why are so many customs taken from the Hindus?" Maria had asked Kerman.

Kerman had a smile on his face when he answered the question. "I don't know how far it is true, but it is believed that when the Parsees landed in Sanjan, Gujarat in their ship, the Yadava prince of that land sent his messenger with a cup full of milk, saying that his kingdom had no place for these foreigners, just like the full cup. It is said that the *Magi* or *Dastoor*, who was the Zoroastrian priest, put a spoonful of sugar in the cup of milk stirred it in front of the messenger, saying that just as the sugar got stirred in the milk without overflowing the cup and sweetening the milk, so would his people mingle with the natives of Gujarat, adopting their dress, customs and language and sweeten their land. The prince was so moved by the wit and wisdom of these people that he welcomed them into his kingdom. True to their word, the Parsees adapted the customs, language and dress of the Gujaratis."

Maria was impressed with this story and understood the reason behind the Hindu customs among Parsees. Although this story and many versions of it have been floating around among the Parsees, it might very well have been that it was the ruler of Sanjan, who had asked them to adapt to the customs of his land.

Maria learnt that the Zoroastrians were the Aryans who believed in one God, Ahura Mazda, who was the fountain of wisdom, truth, and goodness, after Zarathustra the prophet had preached this to his people. There was said to be a split between the monotheistic Aryans and those who believed in many gods, who were known as the *Mithras*. Mithras came to India in 1000 B.C., while the Zoroastrians stayed in Persia. Prophet Zarathustra also preached that the good Lord had an enemy called Ahriman, who was the embodiment of evil. He believed in the existence and friction between good and evil. Initially, Zoroastrianism was known as Mazdayasna, as they believed in Ahura Mazda. Zarathustra preached that all living things had a soul. The good soul was *Spenta Mainyu* and the bad soul was *Angra Mainyu*. Maria was eager to learn and understand the religion of her husband and her children. Since her mother-in-law knew very little English, she learnt most of the Zoroastrian teachings from her sister-in-law and her priest friend. Her sister-in-law was very proud of her religion and told her that the early Zoroastrians came to India in the seventh century when the Arabs invaded Persia and forcibly converted them to Islam. Then many more Zoroastrians came to India in small groups during the following years.

As the days progressed, Maria saw her sister-in-law praying with her head covered with a scarf. Kerman told her that both men and women had to cover their heads while praying, during ceremonies, and inside the Fire Temple. She had seen Kerman wearing a special cotton tunic, which was called the *Sudreh* and tying a thread—called the *Kusti*—around his waist with reef knots after a shower and before going to bed. He used to also recite some prayers while tying this thread. Kerman had explained to Maria that this tunic and thread was introduced to every child before they reached puberty, during an initiation ceremony called the *Navjote*. The ideal age for a boy was nine and a girl, seven. Their daughter was only two years old and had five more years before the Navjote. The rest of the extended family did their *Sudreh–Kusti* with great fervour, every morning and night. The men wore caps on their heads while praying. The caps worn by Zoroastrian men are similar to those worn by the Muslims and larger than those worn by Jews.

This initiation ceremony, which is known as Navjote in India, is called *Sadre Pooshi* among the Iranian Zoroastrians. It is only after this ceremony that a Zoroastrian child is obliged to offer prayers and follow the rituals and customs of their religion. According to what Maria had observed during the Navjote, the ceremony consisted of three main parts: the *Nahan* or the sacred bath which was performed before the ceremony as a cleansing ritual, the ceremony itself when the child wears the Sudre and Kushti, and Ashirvaad or the final blessing. At that time, the child is reminded of the importance of good thoughts, good words and good deeds for his or her salvation. The child is on her or his own journey of salvation. The parents have a duty to encourage and guide their children through their example. A great big party follows after the ceremony to announce the initiation of the child, with dinner and drinks, and the child is given presents, which are usually in the form of gold ornaments or cash. The Zoroastrians add an extra rupee or a dollar for the amount they give, as good luck. The greetings are written in red ink as opposed to black or blue. This too is considered to be a good omen. Another interesting ceremony is the "Sari Ceremony," performed soon after the girl gets her first period. She wears a sari for the first time and that is celebrated in great pomp and splender, too. Sometimes, the elder sister's sari ceremony and younger brother or sister's 'Navjote,' is performed on the same day.

During the years that followed, Maria learnt and observed many more things. Her sister-in-law also explained to her that the prayers were written and recited in a language called the *Avastan*, as that was the oral language of the Persians at the time of Zarathustra, which was the sixth century B.C. All prayers till the first A.D. were passed on through oral tradition. The first written work was in the language called *Pahlavi*, a sister language of Sanskrit. However, these books were destroyed by Alexander when he conquered Persia and burnt all their libraries. It was then Maria understood why the Persians (Parsees) were so bitter and angry with Alexander and called him "Alexander the Curse," and not "Alexander the Great." She also understood why some of them were angry with Islam, the religion that forced many to flee their motherland. Once it was known that Pahlavi and Sanskrit were sister languages, the Zoroastrians were able to translate their prayers in English and Gujarati. Although the kids have to memorize the Navjote prayers in the original language, they are able to understand their meaning.

As the years went by, Maria understood more about this great religion. The very core of Zoroastrianism, as her husband had told her, was based on "Good thoughts, good words and good deeds." Although bad thoughts do flood our minds sometimes, we have a definite choice about what we say and what we do. These choices that we make, they believed, can ultimately make heaven or hell for us on earth. Zoroastrianism is based on *Asha* or *Karma* which says that a man is rewarded according to his actions or deeds. They believe that Ahura Mazda is the creator of heaven and Earth, night and day. The virtues that emanate from Ahura Mazda are justice, truth, righteous thinking, and devotion to God. Though the Zoroastrians fled to India in the seventh century, they renewed their contact with the remaining Zoroastrians in Iran, the Gabars.

The holy books of Zoroastrianism are the *Gathas* and the *Avesta*. They were originally dictated by Zarathustra, the prophet. It is believed that the Persian Empire, which once spread from Azerbaijan to parts of Turkey and Afghanistan, was the seat of Zoroastrianism.

Maria also realized that there were prayers for every occasion and every event. There were prayers for thanksgiving, good health, prosperity, happiness, long life and for the souls of the dead. There was also certain time when these prayers had to be recited. There were prayers that could be recited by individuals, and those that had to be performed only by the priests. *Jashan* was one such prayer ceremony conducted by the priest, with fire burning in the centre of the living room. Jashans were conducted yearly in many houses to invoke blessings or as a thanksgiving for the blessings already being enjoyed by the family. Maria had soon learnt some of the prayers, and she was also allowed to take *loban* or incense to all the rooms of the house with her head covered with a scarf. This was done for the purification of the house. In India, sandalwood was used in the place of incense.

Kerman would look at her and smile with pride and gratitude for having won his family and for being a part of them. She remembered how her sister-in-law and mother-in-law had told her that she could not attend the Jashan ceremony in their apartment, as she was not one of them. When Kerman had heard about it, he was quite upset and took her for a movie instead, and thus both of them did not attend the Jashan. Then on, they had never excluded Maria from the ceremony.

Fire was regarded as holy and the Parsees prayed to *Ahura Mazda* (spirit) through it. Besides fire, the Earth and water were also regarded holy and hence were not to be polluted. Her brother-in-law had told Maria that the Parsees brought the fire from Persia when they came to India, and the first fire temple was built with this fire in the centre of the holy place. Maria did not know how far it was true. It must have been a real challenge keeping the fire alive from Persia to India. A priest had also told her that fire from lightening could have been used to build the first fire temple. The fire in every temple, had to be kept alive at all times and one priest is in charge of the fire.

There was a priest class among the Parsees just like the Hindus. Only a priest's son could become a priest. In order to become a priest, he had to live in the *Madressa* or the training school for six months to a year to learn all the rituals and ceremonies, memorize extensive texts, and get training in *Avestan* and *Pahlavi* so that these candidates would be able to pronounce all the prayers properly. Maria also learnt that a priest's wife was regarded with higher esteem than the wives of ordinary Parsees. She was also addressed differently than the rest of the wives during prayers, and was expected to adhere to rituals more strictly. The male child in the priestly family, had a choice as to whether he wanted to become a priest and go through the required training or not. In Iran, however, the Zoroastrian women are also allowed to become priests.

There was a taboo about women's period. They were not allowed to pray, cook, or sometimes even sleep with their husbands. If the house was big enough, they would go to a different room or sleep on the floor. This varied from house to house. Maria remembered how her mother-in-law had forbidden her to be in the kitchen for those five days a month. Maria just took all this in stride and did as she was told. She had food given to her in a different plate, which was stored in a different place and was never mixed with the other plates. She just enjoyed the rest for five days and did not go into battle with her mother-in-law, who was just following the rules of her religion. Living in the boarding school with students belonging to different religions did help her adapt to the customs of the Parsees. Many of these customs and rituals are not followed by Parsees who are living in the western world.

Being a Christian, she was not allowed to enter the Fire Temple. A non-Zoroastrian in India was (and is) not only forbidden from entering the fire temple, but also forbidden to even see the face of her husband or child if they ever died before her. That would be the hardest thing for any wife or mother. However, in Canada, these rules are not followed so rigidly.

Maria, was not forbidden from practising her religion. In fact, her mother-in-law looked after her children when she went to church on Sundays. Most of the Parsees had no inhibition about either going to church or to a Hindu temple, as they respected and bowed their heads to all prophets, just like the Hindus.

The charitable Zoroastrians not only looked after their own, but also took good care of those who worked for them. They were indeed some of the most caring and generous bosses to work for. They looked after their workers with good pay and lot of benefits, which included free university education for their children. There were many instances where Zoroastrian masters had left a substantial amount of their estate to their faithful maids and other servants. If there was one group of people in India that no one hated or even disliked, they were the Parsees.

The Zoroastrians are a minority in India. In order to maintain the purity of their race, they had to marry within the small community that migrated from Persia. As a result, many rare diseases are perpetuated among themselves. Many of them sometimes seemed eccentric. Maria remembered once when she called her husband "crazy" because of what he was arguing about; he had jokingly replied, "That is true, Maria. A normal Parsee is yet to be born." From then on, Maria always teased him about that. Living in the extended family of her husband, Maria soon realized that living in a extended, or joint-family, as it was called in India, had its merits and demerits.Once you learnt to adapt and accept, the positives outweighed the negatives.

The Zoroastrians are a small community of about 150,000 people in the whole world, most of them being in India and the rest in North America, England, Australia and a few in Iran. Their policy of non-conversion, one or two children per family, and more interfaith marriages are some of the causes for their dwindling numbers. There are also many bachelors and spinsters among Zoroastrians (Parsees), which does not help in increasing their numbers, either. Maria smiled to herself, reminiscing about the days when two mothers from the Bagh had come to her complaining that their sons wanted to marry Christian girls; when they had objected, all their sons said was, "Is not Aunty Maria a good lady? Has she not adapted to our customs? Don't you like her? Why then can't we marry a Christian girl?"

They had teased her and said, "Look what you have done, Maria. You have won the hearts of our youth and given them the courage to marry a Christian. My husband and I had no answer. We just smiled and gave our consent to their marriage."

The Parsees are a fun-loving people who love to party, eat, and drink. They will find an excuse to party and celebrate. "Live and let live" was and is their motto. They are one of the most westernized and affluent people in India, mainly because they look after their own. They are also great philanthropists, which is not in the true character of the rest of the Indians. They have also established many charities and scholarships for non-Parsees in India.

Parsees in India are known for their contribution to education and art (J.J. School of Art, Jehangir Art Gallery), science (Homi Bhabha – a Nuclear Scientist), entrepreneurship (Tata, Wadia and Godrej) and humanitarian values. Zubin Mehta, Freddy Mercury (Freddy Balsara), Rohinton Mistry, and

Bollywood choreographer Shiamak Davar are some of the famous Zoroastrians connected with the art world.

The British were quite fond of the Parsees, and many of them were knighted during the British Raj. Kerman had told her that about sixty-three Parsees were knighted, up till 1946, in India. She remembered three of them: Sir Jamshedji Tata, Sir Pherozesha Mehta, and Lady Jijiboy. If there was one group of people that mourned the departure of the British from India, those were the Parsees. Queen Victoria's picture still adorns many of the Parsee homes, even to this day.

The Parsees considered anything dead as *nasu* or unclean, including cut nails and hair. Nails and hair had to be cut during the day and properly disposed of. They were obliged to wash their hair after a haircut. The dead body therefore had to be disposed as quickly as possible. Since the dead body was unclean, it could not be in the sacred earth, cremated in the sacred fire, nor could it be thrown in the sacred water. Therefore they placed the bodies in the Tower of Silence for a sky burial. Here the bodies are exposed to nature and the vultures. By adapting sky burial, the Zoroastrians were fulfilling the central teaching of their religion, which was to practice good deeds. They were becoming food to God's creatures, even after death.

No living Parsee or non-Parsee is allowed to go to the Tower of Silence, except for two designated men who are known as *Naseh-salars,* or corpse-bearers. Kerman had also told her that what was left of the body after the vultures had their fill would either slide or would be thrown into the well in the centre where it would be dissolved in the limestone. During the monsoons, this water mixed with the remaining pieces of bone and limestone, would be thoroughly filtered in the filtration system in the well, and only clean water entered the deep soil. Though now there are taller buildings surrounding the tower in Bombay, there has been no complain about the stench of any kind because of the scientific way of this burial system. There are only two such towers in the world—one in Mumbai (Bombay was changed to Mumbai in 1995) India, and one in Yazd, Iran. The one in Iran has been out of commission for a very long time. Outside India, the Zoroastrians bury the dead.

Living with the Parsees had widened Maria's outlook on life itself. Their generosity, their zest for life combined with their respect for other prophets and religions made Maria respect and admire these people and question her own narrow-minded belief. By now Maria had a different take on the Catholic religion she had been raised in. Jesus Christ still remained her hero and her inspiration. She loved the wisdom she saw in his parables. However, Christianity was now very different to her than the ritualistic religion she once followed blindly. She believed that a true Christian was one who could forgive till it hurt, love even those who did not love them, believe in the plan of the Almighty even when things seem desperately hopeless, and treat everyone with love and respect no matter who they are and what they have done—in the same way that Jesus treated the Samaritan woman, the tax collectors, and the prostitutes. The few quotations that stuck in Maria's mind were "hate the sin, but not the sinner," "judge not others, so that God may not judge you," and "love thy neighbour as thyself."

Maria realized that each religion had its principles, which if followed, would make this world a better place. No single religion had the monopoly for the way to salvation. This change was brought about after living with Kerman. Kerman had once pointed out to her that her Bible says that "The Kingdom of God is within you." If that is true, why look for heaven somewhere else? Living with the Zoroastrians had liberated her mind from the narrow definition of what is good and bad and what is right and wrong, and opened it to embrace all people as children of one God, Spirit, or Almighty Power—and all religions as an attempt to understand the supreme being and bring meaning and purpose to the lives of its followers.

Maria had travelled a long distance with these noble people, and this journey with them had enriched her life. Though she had been in three different countries with Kerman, her most cherished memories were that of the Bagh, and the love and acceptance of the Parsees towards her during her stay with them.

Chapter 10

STORY OF THE CLOISTER NUN

Time passed by, and the friends met again. Meena's journey, from the time she landed in Canada the first time to meet her husband, till now, had been quite interesting. She was aware of all the decisions she had made and the consequences she had to face, because of them. Meena had found her inner peace and was happy both with her personal and her professional life. She had adjusted well to the Canadian way of living. She looked confident, smart and stylish in her new outfit. She was ready and eager to meet her friends.

Anna's mother wished to go to Poland and India before she died. Anna decided to oblige her mother's wish to go to Poland, soon, as this was as good a time as any other. This would also give her a break from Sam and afford her a chance to think about their relationship. She phoned Sam to tell him about the trip before she told her friends.

"Are you running away, Anna? How long will you be gone?"

"I am not running away. I'll only be gone for two months. I need to think about us, Sam. I want to do what is right for both of us. There is no point in hanging on to each other if we are not ready and unable relocate, or accept the sacrifices and commitment involved in a long-distance relationship. It should not financially or emotionally tax either of us. I am an intelligent adult and I want to take your needs into consideration."

"What about your needs?"

"All human beings are not the same. What is fine for me is not necessarily fine for you."

"I really don't like the fact you are going away, but I understand you are doing it for your mother. I'll email you as often as I can. I love you and always will."

"Thank you, Sam. I love you, too."

Anna felt good with her decision. She wanted to share this with her friends and watch their reaction. She dressed quickly and drove to 'The Red Lobster.' As she was getting off, she saw Maria park her car. They walked in together to find Meena seated at their table.

They greeted each other with warmth. Meena had a wise and calm look and her friends knew that all was well with her. Once they were seated, Meena turned to Anna.

"What's the news Anna?"

"The news may surprise you. I am leaving for Poland with my mother next Saturday, to fulfill her wish. I'll be gone for two months."

"What a coincidence. I am going on a trip to India within a few days, too." Added Maria

Meena was quite surprised with this news.

"Why, Maria?"

"Since I want to write my book, I need to visit India again. Perhaps this would be my last visit. I want to bid my goodbyes to places and people associated with Kerman."

"Why are you going now, to Poland, Anna?"

"My mother is not getting younger and she cannot go alone, so I am taking her."

"What about Sam? How would he feel about it?"

"What about him? He already knows. Although he was not happy about it, he has accepted it."

"Perhaps that explains your pensive mood."

"I have this gut feeling that something is going to happen to me or Sam when I'm away."

"Nothing is going to happen. Enjoy your holidays and don't worry about anything. Remember that we will always be there for you."

"I have this gift of premonition—or shall say curse? I had once dreamt that a distant cousin of mine had gone blind and I was pushing his wheelchair. Do you know that it came true? That same cousin has got glaucoma and is losing his eyesight. I can name a few other incidents like that. That's why I am worried."

"Remember that nothing happens without a reason. Besides, worrying doesn't stop things from happening nor make them happen. 'What next?' should be your response when things happen."

Anna felt a little reassured and calm. Maria was right. There was nothing she could do to stop events from happening. She decided to make the best of her trip with her mother. After their last trip to Quebec, they had not been on any other holiday together. She turned her attention to Meena, who looked the happiest.

"Things must be moving in the right direction for you, Meena."

"That's true. Ramesh is sticking to his commitments and it has been months since he touched his last drink. I am truly proud of him."

"Maria and I never thought that Ramesh would come around, and that things would improve so dramatically. It was incredibly bold of you to leave him in a new country with two dependent boys. More incredible is the fact that you are now helping him to change."

"Don't forget, I had you to guide and support me. You guys were also ready to help me financially if I needed that. What else could I have asked in a friend? You were my family here in Canada. And now, both of you are going on a holiday, and I will miss you."

"You won't be alone, Meena. You are rebuilding your life with Ramesh. You will be perfectly alright. We will email you regularly. Keep us posted."

Anna was in a good mood now. Her friendship with these two Indian friends had been very educational and inspiring. She had learnt a lot about India from them, and yet she always had more questions.

"Maria, since you were born in the forties, do you remember how it was when you went to school during the post-British era? Was there a backlash on Christians?"

"I remember some things. There was a kind of anger about everything British, like the dress, language and religion. Our western names didn't help either.

"By the way, why do you have western names?"

"Anna, that's because the Portuguese converted our ancestors; whoever converted our families, gave us their last names."

"That wasn't right, was it?"

"No, it wasn't, mainly because by erasing our last names, they erased our castes which are so important in India. Hindu Indians had a hard time accepting us. I understand changing our first names, but not the last names. For the longest time we were told by the priests that every Christian had to have the name of a saint as their first name. Since all saints were western, we ended up having western first names. As the time went on, many Christians started using Indian first names. Many went back to their roots and started using even their ancestral last names. As per the backlash, there wasn't any against Indian Christians. Nehru, our first prime minister, ensured that this sort of thing did not happen not only to Christians, but also to all other minorities. Although Nehru was a Hindu Brahmin by birth, he was less religious and more spiritual. I remember him saying, "Humanity is my religion and work is my prayer." He was a very proactive, charming, and caring man. Children addressed him as 'Chacha Nehru,' which meant 'Uncle Nehru.' He started, 'Children's Day,' and also had places reserved in railways, government jobs, and universities for minorities, Anglo-Indians and low-caste Hindus. He was very modern in his way of thinking and very broadminded."

"Who were 'Anglo-Indians'?" Anna asked.

"Anglo-Indians were people of British descent who were either born in India or had one parent or grandparent who was Anglo Saxon. Since the latter were shunned both by the English as well as the Indians, they went through some tough times, especially after the British left. As a result, many migrated to England and other Commonwealth countries. Those who did not wish to leave or could not afford to move out were thus protected."

"After the British left, the medium of instruction in schools changed from English, to vernacular language. Unlike my mother who studied in the English medium, I started study-ing in the vernacular medium. There was only one period of English from grade six to ten. That caused a lot of problems, because all of a sudden from grade eleven through university, everything was taught in English."

"What do you mean by vernacular language? Do you mean Hindi?"

"No, Anna. Hindi and English are our official languages. Though more people in India understand Hindi, they all do not speak it."

"Wow! I did not know that. I thought all Indians spoke Hindi."

"No, we don't. Not only does the language differ from state to state, but also the script. India has twenty-three languages, about ten distinct scripts and more than two hundred dialects. English and Hindi are India's two official languages."

"I really am amazed!"

"That is why we are said to have "Unity amidst Diversity."

"The government of India, soon gave schools the choice to switch back to the English medium of instruction. As a result, Meena and some of my younger siblings were able to study in the English medium. Coming back to life as a Christian, it was not at all difficult in the small South Indian town of Mangalore. There was no animosity against the Christians, especially because of the educational institutions they ran. The best schools and colleges, those days, were run by the nuns or the Jesuit priests. The non-Catholics liked sending their children to Catholic schools, because of the discipline, manners, the English language, and the moral values taught. Even the matrimonial advertisements carried more weight when it was mentioned that the girl was 'Convent Educated.' As far as I can remember, there was absolutely no tension in the school in spite of students of all religions being in my class. We knew of each other's festivals and respected them. Hindus were especially tolerant and respectful of all religions.

"We had neighbours who were Hindus and Muslims. During Christmas, my family would send Christmas sweets to them and during Eid and Diwali, they would send their sweets to our house. We all lived in harmony and peace. The students joked about each other's religions. The Hindus said that the Catholics sinned as much as they wanted during the week and then went for confession and all was pardoned. The Catholics replied that the Hindus sinned all their lives and dipped themselves in River Ganges and all their sins were washed away. The Muslims again had to go to Hajj to atone for their sins. Then we all laughed and were friends again. Life was good."

"What about the other religions?" Anna asked.

"There were some Jains in Mangalore, but no Sikhs, Parsees, or Jews. The Jews were in Bombay and Kerala, the neighbouring state to ours. The rumour was that there was one Persian Zoroastrian family in the town of Mangalore who owned the Persian Bakery. They had one daughter, Zarine. She was extremely beautiful and attended the convent school. She was very fascinated by the nuns and especially one particular nun, whom she worshipped. This Sr. Angelina was exquisitely beautiful and talented, and Zarine could not understand how such a young and good-looking woman could become a nun and consecrate her life to God. She started learning more about Christianity and fell in love with the idea of becoming a bride of Christ, as the nuns were addressed. The religious fervour in her heart became so intense that she decided not only to convert herself to Catholicism, but also join the order of 'Cloistered Nuns.'"

"What is that?"

"The cloistered nuns do not see the world; once they join the convent, they never come out of those walls."

"Till they die?"

"Yes, Meena. Only two nuns are assigned to have any contact with the outside world, and that too, is through a grilled window. These nuns follow the strictest rules; once a girl joins this order and takes her final vows, it is almost impossible to get out. We were told that they have to get special dispensation from the Pope to get out. You can imagine the shock and horror these nuns would experience if they suddenly came out and saw the world after forty or fifty years! Some of these old nuns might not have even seen a motor car when they had joined the convent. This incident devastated the Persian Zoroastrian family. They tried their best to dissuade their daughter, but failed. It is said that the sorrow it caused them made them hate the place, and soon they moved out of the town. As my mother once said, 'For them, their daughter was dead.'"

"Where did they go?"

"They went to Bombay where most of the Parsees lived."

"I would have been equally upset if my daughter joined this order of nuns, even though I am a Catholic."

"Yes, Anna. I can understand the wrath of these parents towards the Catholics."

"Do you know what happened to the girl?"

"I came to know about the identity of this girl, only after my marriage to Kerman and my return from the United States to India. It was providence or coincidence that, after my return from the U.S.A., I started working in a private school owned by rich Hindus, whose principal was a Parsee. When she came to know that I was from Mangalore, she was quite happy. She called me to her office one day and asked if I was going to Mangalore soon. I told her that every summer I take my children to my hometown. She then asked me if I could deliver a letter to a nun in the cloistered convent. I was truly surprised at this request."

"'Of course I will,' I told her, 'but I am a little confused. Who is it that you want me to deliver this letter to?'

'That is a long and sad story of our family. I have an aunt there,' she explained. It was then that she told me the whole story."

"What are the odds that you should land in that school, Maria. Did you meet her?"

"I had never visited this convent before. My friends and I would whisper about the lonely life of the nuns who lived within those high walls. No one dared, nor was curious enough, to climb those walls and peek inside. Little did I know that someday I would be going there. I still remember that day when I went to the convent. I was greeted by a nun who stood behind a screen window and asked me what I wanted. I said I wanted to meet Sr. Theresa, as her niece had asked me to meet her and give her a letter. She told me that the rules did not permit her to see me, but she would be glad to give her the letter. When I asked her if I could return for a reply, she told me that Sr. Theresa was bedridden with rheumatoid arthritis and was not able to write. She told me that Sr. Theresa was in severe pain and was in fact blaming herself for having abandoned her own ancient religion and converting to Christianity. She felt that God was punishing her. When I heard this, I felt very sad for the nun and was worried as to how this news would affect my principal."

"How did your principal take it?"

"She was devastated and very sad."

"That was indeed a sad story," said Meena who was listening quietly.

"How much of your book is finished, Maria?"

"I am half-way through. It may take a long time before it is polished and ready for publication. I may need your help in this."

"Send us both a copy of each chapter as you complete it. By the way, thanks for emailing me your chapter on Zoroastrianism. I loved it"

"You are welcome, Anna."

"Email it to me too, Maria. I would also like to know more about the Zoroastrians."

"I will."

Time was up and they had to leave.

"If I don't see you both before you leave on your respective trips, I wish you a safe journey and enjoyable trips."

The friends decided to email regularly and meet after Maria and Anna returned from their holidays.

Anna had not been to Poland for many years. Her first and last visit was with her husband when they were just married. This time, she was going to see Poland through her mother's eyes and meet her parents' surviving family and friends. She decided to phone her children and tell them about her trip. Anna's mother was very excited. Anna's brother booked the tickets for them and paid for his mother's ticket.

Soon the day of their departure arrived and Maria drove Anna and her mother to the airport, as she was leaving few days later.

"Keep me posted. Tell me the details of your return flight when the time nears. I'll come to pick you both up from the airport, as I am returning earlier. Don't forget to get me a picture of the 'Black Madonna.'"

"Will do, my friend. Thanks for everything."

Chapter 11
MEENA'S TRIUMPH

The year was 2005. Since Anna and Maria had left, Meena started concentrating on her relationship with her husband, Ramesh. She was getting closer to Ramesh again. The boys were happy for her as he was nothing like he used to be. The boys had met him a few times for dinner. His only son from his first wife was also glad that his father was becoming a changed and better person. Meena accompanied him to AA, whenever she could. Ramesh was once again a great man to be with. His positive energy and his knowledge made him a desirable person to talk to, even at parties. Meena was enjoying life on her terms. She started seeing him regularly on weekends. Together they had rekindled the flame they once enjoyed. They had become more attentive to each other. There was once again joy and harmony in her life. Ramesh had realized what he had lost when Meena left and was doing all that he could to win her back. Little did he realize that in the bargain, he was helping himself and improving his own life. Her older boy was planning to apply to Medical School and the younger one was already in the U.S. She was proud of her boys. She emailed to tell her friends about Ramesh and herself. They realized that Meena was a wise and brave lady with determination and perseverance. Her faith in love had helped her to win back the husband she respected and loved.

Maria and Anna had returned from their respective trips, and years passed by. Meena was a proud mother of two extraordinary sons and was the wife of a loving husband. It was the year 2010. Meena's elder son, Ravi, had finished his M.D. and was in his first year of residency to become a cardiologist, which would be another six years of study. Ravi was already twenty-six years old and there was pressure from his grandparents and uncle to get married. They would have liked for him to go to India and choose his bride. However, Ravi had set his heart on an Italian girl, Susan, who was studying with him. She too had finished her M.D. and wanted to start her practice after her residency. She was a nice girl from a good Catholic family, and Meena was determined to let her son choose his own bride when the time came. She would take the responsibility of convincing her in-laws back home. Susan's parents were not very open to the idea of their daughter marrying an Indian boy, but once they met Ravi and came to know him, they accepted him. Ravi was respectful, ambitious, and smart, and was on his way to becoming a cardiac surgeon. Above all, he loved their daughter with all his heart and would take good care of her.

Her twenty-four-year-old son, Raj, had graduated from Stratford, had worked for two years, and was doing his M.B.A. at Harvard University. Things could not have been better for Meena. She had given love a second chance and won her love, back. They had a little celebration when she and Ramesh got back together. Her sons could not believe the difference in Ramesh. "Hats off to our mother," they said. Ramesh's son

Jeevan also was present at this celebration. He came to Meena with sheepish eyes and said, "I was quite mad at you when you left dad after just three years. I was convinced that you married my father just to come to Canada. I am very sorry for having thought so. My dad told me that you are the reason he started going to AA and it was your support and encouragement that helped him kick his addiction. Thank you very much."

"You are welcome. Don't forget that I love your father."

As Ravi wanted to marry his Italian sweetheart, Meena went to India to break the news to her in-laws—and also to do the wedding shopping. After the initial disappointment, they accepted the news, on condition that there would be a Hindu wedding ceremony. Meena agreed to it as Susan had told her that she would agree to a Hindu ceremony as long as they also had a church wedding. Her whole extended family wanted to come to Canada for the wedding. They wanted to buy jewellery to present to the bride. Meena told them that Susan, her would-be daughter-in-law, would appreciate something delicate, unlike the heavy jewellery worn by the Indians. They took Meena with them to select the type of jewellery Susan would like.

The wedding took place, with all the grandeur, in Canada. Both Maria and Anna attended the wedding. Meena lent one of her saris to Anna. She looked gorgeous in a turquoise blue sari. The wedding expenses were shared by the two families. Ravi's expense was paid by her in-laws. Meena's parents sent a handsome amount as wedding present, for their eldest grandson. There was food from both cultures and Bollywood dancing. The Indian women came in all their finery and jewellery, and the Italians with their lovely gowns and dresses. The bride had a white gown for the church ceremony and part of the reception, and then changed into red and gold Indian outfit. She looked beautiful. What made the young girls and men envy this couple most, was the love they had for each other.

Meena's younger son Raj continued his studies in the States, finished his M.B.A., and decided to move back to India to take on the family business with his cousin. His cousin was overjoyed to hear this, as it was becoming very difficult to handle all the demands of their growing business, alone. Besides, his father was getting old. Raj also agreed to an arranged marriage as long as he got to date the girl at least a few times before giving an answer. This would allow him to know what she wanted in life, what her expectations were, and what her stand was on important issues, such as; religion, children and a woman's role in life. After a few dates with different girls, Raj found what he was looking for, and agreed to marry Kiran. She was a foreign-educated girl with the knowledge of western culture, but was glad to settle in India. Her name, Kiran, meant "ray" and she did bring a ray of sunshine into Raj's life. Ravi, Susan, and Ramesh, went to India for the celebration. Just a year after his brother's wedding, Raj was married to Kiran. Meena had gone earlier with Raj.

Meena would have loved for Maria and Anna to come for the wedding. Anna, however, had lost the enthusiasm to travel after her trip to Poland, and Maria had started getting arthritis in her knee and hip joints. Hence they politely declined the invitation. The wedding was in the month of October, which was the perfect weather for a wedding, in Gujarat. Meena's in-laws had a large house with servants to tend to their needs. Cooking, however, was the responsibility of Meena's sister-in-law. The servants helped in cutting the vegetables, grinding the spices, etc.

Ramesh, Ravi, and Susan arrived in the late hours of the morning. They had endured a very long journey from Toronto to Gujarat, and were quite exhausted. Susan was welcomed with warmth and affection. As she entered the house with her husband Ravi, they threw rice on their heads, put a red mark on her forehead, and presented her with money, sari, and jewellery, as she was coming to her husband's ancestral home for the first time. Susan was quite touched by their affection and generosity. Susan bent down and touched the feet of her husband's uncle and aunt as per the Hindu custom. They welcomed Ramesh with equal warmth. Meena's brother-in-law took an instant liking to this knowledgeable man. After bath and a hot vegetarian meal, they all went to bed, though it was only four in the evening. As soon as they lay their heads on their pillows, they were fast asleep.

Ravi, Susan and Ramesh woke up to the melodious duet of the koels. It had been a very long time since Ravi and Ramesh had heard this song, and for Susan it was the first time. It was the most beautiful song she had ever heard. Ravi told her about this evasive bird which was heard, but rarely seen.

"The male koel, though fully black, has a yellowish-green bill and crimson eyes, which distinguishes it from a crow. The female koel is dark brown in colour and heavily spotted and barred with white. Although, she is prettier, he has a better tune."

These birds, oblivious to the world, were singing their love song. Susan got up from the bed and went out. Meena's in-laws had a huge garden. There were parrots, crows and sparrows, but no sign of the koel. No matter how much Susan tried to look in the direction of its song, she was unable to spot the koel.

"You sneaky birds! You know just how to entice us with your melody and then go into hiding. It is not fair. Please show yourself."

Lo and behold! At that very moment, she saw the koels—both male and female!

"Thank you, birds! You have made my trip to India worth it, already. Everything else will be a bonus!"

Susan then went inside the house to have her bucket shower, where the water is kept ready in buckets with a container, to pour it on the body. Meena had instructed Susan about the process, on the previous day. Soon, she was ready for breakfast. This was not the ordinary Canadian breakfast. There were no eggs, toast, cereal or waffles. What she ate was fresh, tasty, and unusual. Then there was chai—tea made with ginger, mint and spices. Once Susan tasted it, she didn't want any coffee—at least until she left Gujarat.

The wedding was another culture shock to Susan. The money they spent and the number of guests who were invited both made her see the disparity between the rich and poor Indians. All gifts were in gold and money. The entire expense of the wedding was borne by the bride, Kiran's family. She was their only daughter, and they were not going to spare any expense for her wedding. Besides, she was marrying a well-educated and very decent young man who would respect and love their daughter and treat her with dignity. Kiran, like Meena, was going to be a working woman, and that was fine with Raj and his family. Susan, being the elder daughter-in-law, was given her due respect and was showered with gifts, even from other relatives, during the wedding. Susan was amazed at the customs and traditions of the Gujarati Indians.

Meena's parents were equally glad to see Susan, Meena, Ramesh and the boys. They too showered them with money and gifts. After the wedding, the couple went on their honeymoon to Kashmir, which is known as the Switzerland of India, and the rest of the family went on a sightseeing trip in Gujarat. On Meena's request, they went to visit Jamnagar, the place where Maharaja lived and the place he had given shelter to the Polish children, including Anna's mother. When she told this to her brother-in-law and the reason why she wanted to visit this place, he was visibly moved. Susan was also interested in visiting the birthplace and house of Mahatma Gandhi in Rajkot. Dhiraj arranged the whole trip. They went to Jamnagar and they saw both the palaces of the Maharaja. She had heard that the camp was close to his summer palace. Meena took pictures of the palaces. This noble deed by the king of Jamnagar had forever tied Poland to India. She saw the rivers Rangmati and Nagmati in Jamnagar and wondered at which riverbank Anna's mother had first spotted Pankaj! She missed Anna and her mother, as they would have loved to visit this place.

"More and more Polish are coming to Jamnagar to see the exact location of the Polish Children's camp. Indians are also visiting Warsaw to visit the school dedicated to Maharaja Jamsaheb Digvijay Singh. What a beautiful piece of history, between two distinctly different cultures and religions!" Dhiraj observed.

Susan was fascinated by the simplicity of Gandhi's residence. His slippers were still next to his bed. Susan took many pictures.

Their sightseeing trip was enjoyable. Everywhere they went, there were friends and relatives who gave them food and shelter. There was always a clean bed to sleep, and fresh hot food to eat. Susan marvelled at the fast pace in which the women made thin wheat rotis that puffed like balloons and were delicious to eat. As you finished one, the other would be on your plate. Susan thoroughly enjoyed the Gujarati vegetarian food.

They returned to Meena's in-laws and then spent a few days with Meena's parents. The warmth and generosity welcomed them wherever they went. Meena's parents were very happy for Meena and Ramesh. They were seeing Susan for the first time as they were unable to attend the wedding due to Meena's mother's heart.

Before they knew, it was time to depart. The newlyweds were also back from their honeymoon. Though Meena felt sad to leave Raj behind, she knew that he was among the people who loved him, and he would visit Canada at least once a year as he had promised. Meena's parents and Dhiraj and his wife invited Susan to visit Gujarat again. Susan had fallen in love with India and wanted to revisit India with her children, when they arrived.

Back in Canada, Meena met her friends and gave them the beautiful silk and brocade saris she had brought for them from her dad's shop. Both Maria and Anna loved them and thanked her for them.

"You'll have to find us an occasion to wear these."

"You both can wear them for the Diwali celebrations, next year."

Meena showed them the pictures she had taken in India. Anna was filled with emotion when she saw the pictures of the Maharaja's palace. She wished she and her mother could have gone to India. She realized that all wishes do not come true.

Once back from India, Meena decided to retire from her nine-to-five-job and start freelancing, as she had turned fifty and had a secure future with Ramesh. He too was advancing in age and wanted to spend the remaining few good years visiting places and doing the things he always wanted to do. Being a student of cardiology, Ravi had advised his stepfather to walk every day for at least half an hour and avoid eating out. Ramesh and Meena started doing just that. Daily walks together, enhanced their communication and brought them closer. Meena had fallen deeply in love with Ramesh. His recovery from alcoholism had been their journey together. Perseverance, faith, and support from each other, had enabled them to rekindle their love. The destination they had reached had been worth the tough journey. As Shakespeare said, "The course of true love never did run smooth."

Chapter 12

MARIA'S CLOSURE

Maria left for India soon after Anna left for Poland. Her visit to India was meant to bring closure to her past and live her life with the memories of Kerman in the celebration of his life. She visited all the places she and Kerman had visited, she walked through the same streets and smelled the air, she spoke to the people who were once their friends, and slept in the same house where they spent much of their married life together. Her in-laws had passed away and her sister-in-law still had Kerman's picture in her old bedroom.

One morning, she woke up at 4:30 a.m. As much as she tried to sleep, she could not. She looked at the picture of Kerman and talked to him.

"Kerman, I hope you know I loved you and will always love you. You will always remain in my heart. However, I want to remember you not with tears, but with joy, celebrating what we once had without regrets or remorse. Yes, there are things I wish you and I had not said and done. We cannot change the past, so let me remember the good things you and I said

and did for each other. Thank you for the love you gave me."
She bid his soul a final goodbye with tears streaming down
her cheeks. She asked him to part without regret or anxiety.
She told him how hard it had been for her to say goodbye to
him and that she had finally come to the conclusion that since
she couldn't bring him back even for a minute, she would
have to release him from her love so that he could continue
his journey. This talk with Kerman gave Maria the closure she
badly needed to continue her life on Earth. She closed her
eyes and felt calm and composed.

Then, she went out and stood at the balcony window
where she had stood numerous times in her life, waiting for
her Kerman to get back from work. She remembered how
glad and relieved she felt each time to see him get out of the
taxi. The memory was still alive in her heart. A pang of deep
pain entered her soul. She would never ever see her Kerman
get out of a taxi and walk home, ever again. Once again, she
felt the finality of separation through death.

The activity on the street, in front of her, caught her attention. A small boy, about eight years old, was zigzagging fast
on the bicycle. She wondered where he was going so fast and
so early in the morning. Then she saw a group of men and
one woman walking. She knew they were going to work by
the urgency in which they walked and the bags in their hands.
They must be going to the railway station, she thought. Then a
group of young girls and boys strolled by; they were walking
leisurely. She instinctively knew that they were on their way
home from the call centre, the much-debated outsourcing jobs
of the night. Then came the empty handcarts pushed by men,
which would be soon loaded with vegetables or other wares to
be sold. Maria stood there, mesmerized by the life in Bombay.

By 6:00 a.m., the first double-decker bus passed by with
more cars, trucks, handcarts, bicycles, mopeds, pedestrians

and motorbikes all finding space on a laneless road. It was nothing short of a miracle how everyone, including the two stray dogs, managed to travel on this road, in both directions, without a single accident or even a brush against any of the others. Vehicles honked, but no one paid any attention. It looked like all traffic rules were violated here, yet there was order amidst great chaos.

Maria's glance then fell on the lone man sleeping on a bed made of newspapers, on the sidewalk, just in front of her window. He was sleeping in his boxers. At exactly 6:30 a.m., he got up, folded his newspapers, and hid them in the groove between the pole of the streetlight and the electric meter box. Then he put on his undershirt, pants and shirt which had been neatly folded and left on the sidewalk, wore his slippers, checked his pockets, put a towel on his shoulder, and quickly went away. *He must be going to some small coffee hut for a wash and breakfast*, thought Maria. Though there was plenty of work in Bombay, there was no affordable place to live. Hence the man had found his bedroom on the sidewalk, which was all he could afford with his meagre means. Maria wondered if he had a family in some village far away from Bombay.

It was already 7:00 a.m. now. The noise on the street was so loud that she could not go back to sleep, even if she wanted to. Her sister-in-law and her nephew were asleep, as they were used to this noise. She brushed her teeth, changed her clothes, and went for a walk in the Bagh.

As she was walking, she looked at the dates on the buildings. The Bagh she was living in, was built by the Wadia family. Buildings read "Rustomji N. Wadia Trust." The earliest date marked on these buildings was 1924 and the latest, 1930. It is said that Queen Victoria lived in a palace next to the Bagh, whenever she visited Bombay, and this land was originally the cemetery for the horses. The Wadia family had bought it from the British and built these clusters of apartment buildings exclusively for the Parsees. Queen Victoria's palace next door was converted into a hospital. Maria had been to that hospital and seen the huge parlour with chandeliers and the winding marble staircases leading upstairs. Nothing of the original glamour was visible. Maria wondered how many beautiful, classy ladies might have descended those stairs, in their beautiful gowns, and waltzed around with distinguished young men. She wondered how many hearts must have found love and how many were broken.

She stayed in Bombay for another two days and travelled to her hometown, Mangalore.

It was the month of September and the monsoons were almost coming to an end. She found the greenery more luscious and clean. She remembered how the leaves of the trees almost looked brown with dust till the first rains in June washed them and exposed their true colours. She remembered the smell of the earth when the first rains touched the parched earth, which craved the touch of water. The earth emitted such a beautiful smell that it seemed that the Earth was crying in satisfaction, gratitude, and pleasure. It devoured the rain water into its insatiable heated body. Each time it rained, the smell diminished, till finally there was no smell and the earth seemed satiated. It had absorbed enough water to cool its body and the excess water then started flowing. Maria remembered walking in this clear rain water running on the stones and pebbles, with bare feet. The water seemed as happy as the earth and they both seem to be dancing with joy. It was such a feat for children to walk barefoot in this rain. Their feet had adapted to the stones by forming a layer of thick skin under their soles. It was common for Maria and her siblings to take their shoes or slippers off while playing in the yard or walking in the rain.

Her little town was changing rapidly. With the urbanization, the crows and sparrows had become less and the tiny squirrels were never to be seen. There were too many people and too many apartment buildings! Mangalore had lost its quaintness. It was now a buzzing city of noise, pollution and too many skyscrapers. It had become a seat of knowledge and education, with colleges springing for every discipline. They were branches of Canadian, American, and Australian universities. Advertisements of these were seen all over the town. The ones who could not afford to travel abroad could get the same education for a fraction of the amount by staying in their own town. There were even Ayurvedic and Homeopathic colleges. This had attracted students from all over India, China, and other countries to her little town of Mangalore.

Her youngest brother had once told her that Mangalore was a dead town, because there were only old people living in it. Thus, the town, which had been abandoned by the young and was called the home of the aged, was now bustling with life, energy and activity of the youth.

With the increased population had come the congestion and dirt. Change is a strange thing—you either accept it by looking at the positive effects or shun it because of its negative effects. Maria wanted to accept the change as it was inevitable. There was no point clinging to the past. Change had brought more construction, more jobs, and more malls to this small town. The prices of properties were going through the roof. The old Mangalore where everyone knew everyone from their community was vanishing fast. She was glad that the Koel was still there with its melodious cry each morning, reminding her of her lost love. Much had happened since Maria was a teenager! She was glad to be back and she was also glad that she was returning to Canada. She had come to the realization that no matter how much she loved her India, her place now was in Canada, her adopted country. India was a place to visit, while Canada was her home.

Maria was in constant touch with her friends. However, she had not heard from Anna for a week and wondered why she had stopped emailing her. *She must be enjoying herself and has found no time for her friend*, thought Maria. She knew that Anna would either call or email her when it was time for her to return to Canada. Maria flew back to Bombay and soon boarded the plane to Canada. She was glad to be going home.

Back in Canada, some disturbing news was awaiting Maria. Anna had postponed her return to Canada. She met Meena and was glad for the progress she was making with her husband. Maria engrossed herself in her writing.

Years passed, and her youngest son found a Polish girl and was married. It was a small and intimate wedding. By the year 2011, Maria had published her book and was busy planning her next project. Though her first book didn't make great waves, Maria was happy with its modest success. She wrote more for pleasure than for money.

Her friendship with Anna and Meena had grown to a higher level through their journey of trials and tribulations. They loved and cared for each other, in spite of knowing the others' weaknesses. They walked beside each other to support, encourage, sympathize, and understand, by holding each others' hands when the need arose. Their friendship was never a hindrance to the other's dreams. As Arnold H. Glasow rightly said, "A true friend never gets in your way unless you happen to be going down." Maria knew that was exactly what her friends had done for her.

Chapter 13

ANNA'S VICTORY

Anna spent her two months in Poland with her mother. Though her mother was already in her eighties, she was still mobile and had her memory intact. She wanted Anna to take her to all the places she had been to as a child. Their first stop was Krakow. Since they had no relatives or friends there, they stayed in a hotel. Here they walked along the 'Royal Route,' and visited Czartoryski Museum and saw Leonardo Da Vinci's "Lady with Ermine." The most disturbing and heart wrenching trip was to the 'Auschwitz Concentration Camp.' After that visit, Anna felt so sad that she could not eat anything that night. *Evil does exist,* she concluded. Their next stop was Warsaw, where they stayed with distant relatives, who had known Anna's mother as a child. They took Anna and her mother to Maharaja Digvijay Singh School. Though the school looked like any other from outside, once you entered it was a different story. The walls were covered with pictures of Indian monuments, landscape, gods and goddesses. Anna wondered where she was! The guide told them that in 1920, the Mahraja had visited his uncle in Switzerland. There he had learnt about Polish history and culture from the Polish neighbours.

"This might have played a small part in welcoming us to his kingdom," observed Anna's mother

Wherever Anna went, she missed Sam and wished that he was there with her. No matter how many people she met and how much fun she had, there was always this void in her heart that could only be filled by the presence of Sam. The distance and the time just convinced her that she loved Sam and she wanted to work something out with him. They were in constant touch through email and phone.

It was almost the end of her holidays; there were only two weeks left to leave Poland. Sam had said that he was eagerly waiting for her return, and was counting the days and hours. Anna was happy that her holiday was coming to an end, and was looking forward to returning to Toronto - and to Sam. Her distant cousin invited them to Szczecin. He wanted to take them to the Crooked Forest of Gryfino, as it was quite close to his place.

After spending a few days with her cousin's family, they went on their trip to this unique and famous forest. Her cousin, Waldek, drove them to this place and they embarked on the journey with great enthusiasm and excitement. This was going to be their last sightseeing trip. She and her mother were both fascinated to see this unique forest bent at the bottom and then straight. It is believed that the carpenters bent them manually through sticks when the plants were tender for the purpose of making certain items. Anna took a lot of pictures of this Crooked Forest. It was a worthwhile trip. They thanked their cousin before sitting in the car.

"Please don't thank me. It was a pleasure."

"Waldek, you should visit Canada and I will take you to all the places in Toronto."

"Thank you. I'll try to come next year."

Sam would have loved to see it, Anna thought. This was a place for those who loved nature and natural beauty. Perhaps someday she would come again with Sam. With these thoughts, Anna closed her eyes. At that very moment, Anna realized that the car was going too fast. Within seconds, it lost control and crashed into a tree. *Is this my destiny or just a freak accident?* This was Anna's last thought before she lost consciousness. When she opened her eyes, she found herself in the hospital.

It had been many days since the accident. Though she had come out of the coma within five days, it took her at least a fortnight to realize where she was and what had happened. She felt extremely uncomfortable, with pain all over her body. Although she had gained complete consciousness, the doctors kept the death of her mother and cousin from her. She was still very fragile and they were scared that she might not be able to take the shock. Anna's children were notified of the accident. Her daughter took compassionate leave and flew to Poland to be with her mother. Neither Sam nor her friends were notified, as no one knew their contact numbers. In the meantime, her relatives had extended her ticket for four months.

"Where is my mother?" was her first question.

Anna was devastated at the fact that her mother was gone forever. She was more saddened by the thought that she never had a chance to say goodbye to her. It was only after her relatives consoled her, saying that she had fulfilled her mother's last wish of revisiting Poland, did she feel a little better. The death of her cousin was also devastating. With what love and care he and his family had looked after them! She felt guilty and responsible for his death.

She learnt that she had broken her legs in three places and she had undergone surgery. The doctors explained to her that one of her legs would be shorter and she would need special shoes to correct the difference in height. Though all these things bothered her, she was glad to be alive. Anna was a determined and resilient woman. She would take whatever came her way. She would do the necessary exercises, and get well soon. She knew that her recovery was not going to be easy and fast. After all, there must be a good reason why God had kept her alive.

Her thoughts then went to Sam. Did he know what had happened to her? Did he try to contact her? It was days before she could get a laptop to check her emails. There were ten emails from Sam. The first few said that he was eagerly waiting for her arrival. Then there were disappointed emails, and the last ones had lost hope. Sam did not know whether Anna had forgotten him, wanted to break up with him, had found someone else or was ill. In the last email he had told her that he was leaving Canada and going to Africa for a holiday where he could just be with nature and paint without any electronic gadgets to disturb and distract him. He said that he needed to do this as he was not sure what had happened to Anna.

It was Anna's fault in a way that she hadn't given him any particular number to call. She called him from her cell and the cell had been off when she was travelling in the car and remained off and was drained of batteries. As she read his emails, tears filled her eyes. She emailed him and did not get an answer. She called him and there was no answer. Then she called her friend Maria, telling her what had happened and about the extension of her trip. Maria felt very sad and at the same time relieved to know that Anna's life had been spared and she was on the mend.

"Please concentrate on getting well, my friend. Don't worry about anything else. My trip was good and it served its purpose."

"Could you do me a favour? If Sam calls, could you inform him of my accident? Yours is the only number he has. I have not been able to catch hold of him."

"He did call. There was a message from him, and I tried to call him back to tell him that I too hadn't heard from you, but could not get him. Get well soon."

Maria felt very sorry for Anna, as she was hurting in body and soul.

Anna felt a bit better after talking to Maria. She was glad that he had indeed tried to find out about her. She had to give him the benefit of doubt. Anna wondered what would Sam have done if he knew the truth? Would he still be by her side through her recovery or leave her? Anna was not able to answer these questions for sure. Going to Africa without knowing what had happened to her, was an escape, she thought. On the other hand, she realized that each human being was different and instead of getting frustrated with a temporarily disabled Anna, she was glad that he had gone far away from her. Yet, there was not a day that passed by that she did not think of him. It is true that "some people quickly come to our lives and quickly go, some stay for a while, and leave footprints on our hearts, and we are never, ever the same"

Sam's story was a sad one. He had been a successful businessman travelling to different Canadian provinces and the U.S. Due to some misfortune he had lost everything when he was just fifty. It was then that he had started painting as a means of expressing his sorrow and frustration. Painting had been his gift and passion, but was set aside due to the lack of time. This new venture, although gave him mental satisfaction, was not enough to earn bread for his family. This naturally created anger and resentment, and soon he was parted from his spouse. Anna had accepted him as he was, because she knew that he had not lost his money due to drugs, alcohol, or gambling. How could Anna hold his poverty against him? Anna prayed daily for Sam's safety and his success. No matter where he was and whom he belonged to, she would always wish him well. That, she knew, was true and unselfish love. It was so much easier not to feel jealous of his women when he was not with her than when they were together.

Besides her legs, Anna had other fractures in her body. She knew she could not return to Canada until she was at least healed to some extent. She could not even stand, let alone walk. After she had lots of physiotherapy and a bit of practice walking with a walker, Anna returned to Canada. It was March of 2006.

The Anna that returned to Canada was a broken woman. She had lost her mother, her cousin, and her love. She wondered why God had kept her. On contemplation, Anna realized that perhaps God knew that she had some unfinished business upon this earth. Perhaps she had more sorrow to bear or more joy to experience. Her mother had once told her, "We are all born with a cup for joy and a cup for sorrow. Once they are full, our journey on this earth will end." This faith in the Almighty's plan and her own resilience made her determined to get up and walk again.

As soon as Anna reached Canada, she did two things: first, she requested her children to help her sell the house and move into a condo, as it would be easier to maintain and resign from her job. Her office gave her a beautiful retirement party. Then she concentrated on recovering fully. In the beginning, she was unable to walk as much or as fast as she did before. Her children took turns driving her to her doctor's appointments and physiotherapy. Maria too helped Anna during weekdays and Meena during weekends. Some Mondays, they would still drive down to their favourite Red Lobster, and have lunch, and continue exchanging their stories. Years passed by, and Anna recovered almost completely. Her new orthotic shoes compensated for the difference in the lengths of her two legs. She had become the old Anna.

The year was 2011. The three friends were quite settled in their lives. Anna was improving in health and mood. Her energy was renewed and she was focussed on her painting. Her walking too had improved considerably after she had started massaging her legs with the Ayurvedic oil given to her by Meena's in-laws, when they had come for Ravi's wedding. Her friends from her office kept in touch with her. They talked of old times and laughed and joked together. Anna was happy at the progress she had made. She was attending to all her personal needs, including driving, shopping and cooking. She was glad she was not dependent on anyone after the accident. She still had much to be thankful for, and she was going to use her faculties to bring some joy to others who needed it. With this thought in mind, she started volunteering in the seniors' home, giving free painting lessons to the elderly who were so inclined. This became her pet project.

Her life seemed meaningful and almost complete. She was starting to enjoy life once again, attending dinners, parties, and outings with her friends. Then, she had her children and grandchildren who visited her often and invited her over. She remembered Sam with fondness and not regret or bitterness. Her heart rejoiced at the memories instead of aching with pain. Whenever she was dejected, she would think of her daring days with Sam and smile to herself. She thought of their travel in his truck across three provinces in the middle of winter. In fact, she was glad and proud of herself for having taken a chance on happiness and would die contented and happy. She remembered their silly chatter, their love of nature, human issues, politics, justice, freedom, and above all, their love. He had carved a special place for himself in her heart and she cherished it. She was sure he had loved her once and that was enough.

"Time and tide waits for no man," Maria always said. All three friends were progressing in age. Anna was sixty-one years old, Maria sixty-six, and Meena had turned fifty. Anna, as usual, took good care of herself. She reasoned that if her body was the temple of God, then she might as well keep this temple presentable. Anna had gained modest fame for her work. She had some good admirers of her work who supported and guided her. Dan was one of them, and she was ever so grateful for all that he had done for her in the most unselfish way. He was her manager and mentor.

It was the thirteenth of September. The next day was her exhibition, and it was the anniversary of the day she had met Sam in person many years ago. She was looking forward to the exhibition of her paintings. Dan had done everything to ensure that the event went on, smoothly. Anna felt grateful for having friends like Maria, Meena, Dan, and Mark in her life. She was indeed a fortunate lady. At that very moment, the phone rang; it was Maria.

"I just wanted to wish you all the best, Anna. I hope many of your paintings get sold tomorrow. Know that you are a very good artist and you have much going for you. You deserve all the success in the world."

"Thank you very much."

"See you at the gallery, tomorrow. Hope Dan is picking you up."

"Yes, he is."

As she put the phone down, she felt a sharp pain in her chest.

Can it be my heart?

She dismissed the thought. She had been experiencing shortness of breath recently, but that was not unusual, especially during the months of April to May, and sometimes September to October, when her allergies were the worst. Some years were so bad that she needed to use her puffers. She sat down and took some deep breaths, and then used her puffers. She felt great relief. She got up slowly and went to the mirror. Her hair was grey now, as she had stopped colouring it since she became sixty. Advancing years and the accident had left their mark on her face and body. Though her hair was almost grey, her heart could still sing like a bird. She thought of the Koel, a bird she so much wanted to see. If it wasn't for her accident, she would have gone to India for Raj's wedding. However, she had heard this mesmerizing song of the koel, on the internet. Deep in her heart there was still a spark that could respond like the female koel, if Sam called her. She felt lighthearted and giddy with excitement, in a way that she could not explain. She told her thoughts to calm down and decided to go to bed early in order to be fresh and ready for the next day.

She woke up with some discomfort at four a.m. on September 14. She tried to go back to sleep, but couldn't. An hour passed, tossing and turning. Finally she got up and went to her balcony. The air was refreshing and cool. She took deep breaths, standing absolutely erect, as advised in yoga. She made coffee and sat in the balcony, sipping her coffee and looking out at the street in front of her balcony. It was five o'clock now. Except for a few cars and a rare truck, and the full moon on the sky, the street was lifeless. There was not a soul to be seen. The scenery was nothing like what Maria had told her about Bombay. The moon would soon fade away with the sunrise. *Would the moon be upset with the sun for making it disappear?* Anna wondered. Perhaps not, as it had its time to shine for the whole night with all its beauty, through the light of the same sun, and be a solace and inspiration for numerous bleeding hearts. Anna compared herself to the moon and Sam to the Sun. She was able to show her beauty through the love and warmth of Sam for a short but significant time in her life.

She had a sudden idea—why not paint this scenery and name it "Void"? She went to her solarium, which she had converted into her studio, and started painting the scene as a reflection of her soul. She could not put a finger on her mood, as her heart was daring to expect a miracle, while her head was ringing a bell of warning and caution. She was so engrossed in her thoughts and work that it took a while for her to realise that the phone was ringing. It was Dan, reminding her to be ready at the appointed time.

Anna took extra care to look presentable before heading to the art gallery. It was a day when all of her old and new pieces of art would be displayed. Her exhibition was advertised in a few local papers. Though Anna had sold some paintings during her previous shows, this by far was the biggest exhibition she had ever had since her accident. Anna was nervous to meet all the important and curious people. Dan came to pick her up for this great day in her life. Dan had become her dear friend, unselfish to the core. He assured her that it was going to be alright. Maria and Meena had many times told her that she would be very happy if she married Dan. Anna somehow could not bring herself to love anyone. She was content and happy with his friendship, and if Dan wanted more, he had never expressed it. Anna had an interesting collection of paintings for display. Her favourite painting, however, was of two lovers stretched on the couch watching the sunset. This painting had so much significance to her life that she did not want to sell it.

"Not for Sale," it said.

She reached the art gallery well in advance. Dan introduced her to the different artists and guests that started coming in. People came to view the exhibition and buy her paintings. Maria, Meena, and Ramesh soon arrived. Anna walked around for a while with them, meeting and greeting everyone, and then sat on a chair as she felt a bit tired. By then, she saw her family walking towards her. All of her three children with their spouses were there to support her. They were proud of their resilient mother and her accomplishments. They came and kissed her.

"You look quite pale, Mom. All this excitement has tired you. You'd better sit here for awhile."

"Thank you, children. I will rest. Meet me before you leave."

This is not like me. I am always so full of energy—but I am more than sixty, after all, and age catches up with everyone, thought Anna.

People who knew her came to congratulate her. She occasionally stood up to greet friends and fellow artists. Soon her children came to wish her goodbye. She hugged each one of them and thanked them for everything they had done for her since her accident. As she was saying this, she became very emotional.

"Mom, you are acting as if we are leaving you forever."

"That's just the sign of old age, children. Goodnight and thank you."

"Goodnight Mom, take care."

It is then that she saw Sam, walking towards the one painting that she did not want to sell. He stood there staring at it for a long time—it was the same tall figure with those dreamy eyes. She could not believe that he could still send the same shivers through her body. A sweet smile crept on his wrinkled face. He looked calm and composed. Anna strained to see if he had come with a woman. There was no one with him. *He could have left her at home,* thought Anna. She wanted to leave before he could see her. It is true that she had wished to see him before she died, and she was glad she had seen him. She wanted nothing more. She would have to take a taxi and leave a note for Dan. She would not give him cause to worry about her, as he cared for her very much. Just as she was about to leave, she saw Sam wipe the tears from his eyes. She knew her painting had touched him. Is it possible that he still loved her? She sat back on her seat. Suddenly, she did not want to leave anymore. Sam had one look at the painting and knew that it was their picture.

"What a beautiful picture!" the words poured out of his mouth involuntarily.

"Did you say something?" a lady next to him asked.

"I was just admiring this picture."

"I love that picture too. It's a shame that it is not for sale."

"The artist must have a good reason for not wanting to sell it. I am looking for the artist. Have you seen her?"

"I saw her walking a few minutes ago. She must be around."

"Thank you."

"You're welcome."

I will find her and ask her for this painting and I know she will not refuse, he thought.

He continued to stare at the picture. Anna had painted this picture of them sitting on the couch. The expression in their eyes said so much. His loving hands were around her waist and hers on the top of his hands. Though they were looking at the sunset, their eyes seemed to be waiting for the sunrise in their lives.

"May I help you, sir?"

"I want to meet the artist who painted this picture; I want to buy it."

Dan was stunned by the determination in this man's voice. "This painting is not for sale, sir. I'll take you to Anna Grebowska."

Anna saw Dan and Sam talking, and soon Dan was bringing him to her. She also saw a mixture of anticipation and anxiety on Sam's face. They were right in front of her now.

"Anna, this man insists that he wants to buy the only painting that is not for sale."

Anna raised her head and looked at her Sam, the only man who was able to overrule her head to win her heart and inspire her to paint. That man, her Sam, was in front of her asking to buy the painting which was symbol of their love. What she felt at that moment was impossible to explain. The joy, excitement, confusion and divine satisfaction crept through her whole being. She turned her head to Dan,

"Dan, you may leave us and look after the sales and I shall deal with this man."

There was tenderness in her speech and Sam noticed it. Dan left as she got up from her chair. The emotions that went through her heart made her lose her balance, and Sam caught her just in time. He held her for a few seconds till she regained her balance and composure.

"How are you, Anna? Is Dan your husband?"

"No, Sam. He is my good and dear friend. What about your wife or companion?"

"I have no wife or companion. At the moment, I am single. By the way, I would very much love to buy the painting which is not for sale."

"You can have it, Sam. However, I cannot give it to you now. I have already refused to sell it to two other people. Come home tomorrow, and I will give it to you. Here's my card."

"Thank you. How have you been? I so much want to talk to you. May I take you for lunch tomorrow? I would like to tell you all about my life, my follies and my, should I say, enlightenment? I also want to know about your life and your accident. Above all, I want to beg for your forgiveness. I will understand if you do not want to see me, ever."

Anna looked at him, hesitated for a minute and then said, "Yes. You may take me for lunch, tomorrow."

Sam could not believe his ears. She was too good to him. "Thank you, Anna. Please walk with me and let me see all your paintings." They walked hand in hand, pausing at each picture.

"You are pretty good. There is a positive energy in all your paintings, irrespective of their moods. I remember this one. This was the walk in the park when I visited you in Toronto."

"You are right. Can you guess where this one was painted?" Anna pointed at the painting of a river with the sun setting and lone man sitting on the rock.

"Yes, of course. That is the river in Manitoba when you came to visit me."

"Good memory, Sam!"

They continued to view all the other paintings. Some jolted instant memories in Sam and some needed pausing and reflecting. However, there were some paintings with surroundings and foliage alien to Sam.

"These are beautiful, Anna, but I don't recall visiting these places."

"They were painted after my trip to Poland. I visited the places where my mother was born and lived as a little girl. This is the picture of the Crooked Forest. I have so many questions and so many things to tell, but I'll wait till tomorrow."

All of a sudden, Dan saw Anna her hands clasped tightly in Sam's. There was a new and unusual glow on her face, which he had never seen. He instinctively knew that it was Sam. It was true that he had hoped that they could be more than friends, but once he had known that her love was only for Sam, he had respected it and they had developed a beautiful friendship. His girlfriend Debbie had also accepted this platonic friendship between Dan and Anna. Dan was glad that her Sam had returned at last. He came with his outstretched hand.

"Hello, sir. It looks like you got more than the painting you wanted. I am sure you are Sam. Don't ask me how I know this."

"I would like to know."

"Look at the glow on her face. She looks ten years younger!"

"I am glad I can do this to her!"

"I am glad to have met you. I have to go as the lady next to my desk wants to buy that painting of the Crooked Forest," saying this, Dan left them.

Sam looked at Anna,

"You look pale and tired, my lady. You'd better go home and rest."

"I will Sam. Good night."

"Good night. See you tomorrow."

Anna had always loved the way he called her "my darling lady" "my sweet lady" or "my beautiful lady". Maria and Meena, who were engrossed in one of Anna's painting completed in Poland, also saw Sam as he was leaving. The tall stature and the exquisite features told Maria that it must be Sam.

"It would be such a blessing if it is Sam, Meena. Anna deserves to be happy, at last. I hope he is not married or something. You never know. Let us find out."

They left Ramesh and almost ran to Anna. With one look at her, they not only knew that it was Sam, but also that he was not taken.

"So, my friend, your Sam found you at last. You are beaming with joy, Anna. We haven't seen you this happy in years. It was true love, after all."

"We are glad for you. Why did he run away, so fast?"

"He could see that I am tired and wanted me to rest. He is coming to take me out for lunch tomorrow."

"Good. Have fun. We must be going too."

"Wait. I want to thank you both for everything you have done for me." Saying this, Anna gave them both a hug.

"Oh! Anna, you have already thanked us."

"I will not thank you again. I promise."

Soon, they were gone. Anna had a successful exhibition, she had made a good sale, and then to crown it all, her Sam had come back to her. She felt great. She thanked Dan for his help in arranging this exhibition and told him how fortunate she was to have a friend like him. They wound up and then Dan dropped her home. Dan came to her door and she gave him a hug of affection and gratitude.

"I'll come tomorrow at about six-thirty to settle the accounts. You'd better rest as you have had a hectic day."

"Thanks, and goodnight, Dan."

Anna took a quick shower and went to bed. She had an undisturbed, sound sleep for eight hours, and when she woke up it was already bright. September fourteenth was now etched in stone in her life. Anna got up, brushed her teeth and sat with a cup of coffee on her rocking chair in the solarium. She could see the lovely fall colours from her place. Every part of the scenery seemed to appear more beautiful, and every twitter of a bird more melodious, this morning. Even the coffee tasted delicious. She sat there recalling the events of the previous night.

She always had a shower in the morning, but that day she felt lazy. Where was her energy?

I don't need a shower. I had one last night, she thought. She wore her favourite white dress and waited for Sam. Sam loved ladies in white dresses.

Sam was already at her condo ten minutes before noon. She opened the door, and there he stood with a bunch of red roses in his hand.

"These are for you, my darling Anna. I don't know if I have the right to say that I love you. I love you today even more than I loved you years ago—with greater depth and certainty."

Anna took the roses and just said, "Thank you."

Anna was not going to get carried away. She was too old and frail to get hurt again. She believed him that he loved her at that moment and that is all that mattered. Then he took her in his arms tenderly and with great affection. Anna did not resist. He kissed every part of her face. Anna responded with equal sweetness. She felt dizzy when their lips met. Before they could be swept away by the forces of nature, Sam released her from his arms.

"We have to go for lunch. I have made reservations in a very good restaurant."

Anna remembered how he had done the same when she had gone to see him the very first time. They locked the door and went out. The food was really good at this Italian restaurant. They ate and talked. Somehow Anna was unable to eat much, as she felt full with joy and excitement.

"You said that you wanted answers to many questions. Now is your chance. Shoot."

"When did you get back from Africa and why didn't you contact me then?"

"I got back from Africa in 2007. I read about your accident and did not know what stage you were in and what to expect. Besides, I was in relationship with a woman whom I had met in Africa. We had a few things in common and all was well. It lasted for two years and then we parted, in 2009. I could have contacted you then, but didn't as I was not sure if I was ready for the challenge. Besides, at that time, I needed to be alone, to sort out my feelings and find out what I wanted from life. I was still very restless and felt worthless. I had nothing to offer you or anyone else. I felt depleted and empty. I had to be sure of myself before I took any further steps. Why didn't you try to contact me?"

"Knowing you, I was sure you would be with some woman, and I did not want to come in between the two of you. I also knew that if you wanted, you would find your way back to me. I was only worried if I would be alive till then."

"We are here now."

"Yes. We are."

Nothing seemed to have changed between them. They were quite comfortable and were able to pick up right where they had left, in the most natural way. Sam understood her reasoning for not contacting him. Anna was the type of a woman who would rather die with her love encaged in her heart, than proclaim it when her man was with another woman. Sam knew that she was convinced that such a confession of love, at the wrong time, brought more pain than pleasure to all people involved.

"It is true that my journey has taken me to many places and people, but none gave me peace as you did. I had numerous women in my search for the right one. Each left me more dejected and lost. From time to time, I felt this hollow feeling in my heart, and did not know how to get rid of it. Then one day, it dawned on me that I was the most comfortable being with you, whether it be walking, talking, watching a sunset, or even cooking a meal. The more I thought about you, the more I wanted to see you and talk to you. I want nothing more than what you can offer me.

"What if I was dead?"

"Somehow, I knew you could not be dead. I felt some spirit always with me, especially, when I was down, desperate, or depressed and it lifted me up. Although at that time I didn't realize it, later I knew it was your spirit. Do you remember what you had said before you left for Poland with your mother?"

"What did I say?"

"No matter what happens to our relationship, I will always love you, and my spirit will always be there with you. As you are walking back from work, cold and lonely, if suddenly you feel that some warm wind is encircling you, know that it is my spirit."

"Yes, I do remember. What would be your response if I was disabled?"

"Being the man I am now, nothing would matter."

His hand was now on her hand and they continued to talk.

"If I hurt you in any way, please know that it was not my intention; I apologize. I was not the person I am now. Can you forgive me, Anna, for any pain I might have caused you by my behaviour?"

"Yes. I can. Am I not supposed to forgive seventy times seventy, as a follower of Christ?"

He had a smile on his face.

"That is right. I am glad you are a follower of Christ and a forgiver."

"That feels good coming from a so-called atheist."

They both laughed and continued to eat and talk. Anna told him about her trip to Poland and the places she visited, her accident, loss of her mother and cousin, and her slow recovery; Sam told her about the beauty of nature in Kenya and about Mount Kilimanjaro, which he had climbed.

"After seeing Africa, I am convinced that if there ever was a 'Garden of Eden', then it must have been in Africa. Its natural beauty surpasses any that I have ever seen. If you see some of my paintings, you will know that what I say is true. Someday we will go back there."

"God willing, we will."

"What is the Muslim saying that meant, 'God willing'?"

"It is *Insha'Allah*."

"How did you learn that, Anna?"

"I had a lawyer friend who worked in Dubai for some years, and she used to say it."

"Was she a Muslim?"

"No. She was English, but she liked the saying very much and used it often. I've been using it too, as it makes complete sense."

They finished their lunch in leisure and went back to Anna's place. Sam kissed her and was about to leave when Anna felt the strong urge to hold him. Her premonition told her that she may not see him again. She impulsively asked him to lie beside her, just as she had once asked her late husband, Adam. If Sam hesitated, it was just for a second. He obeyed her and held her close to his outstretched body. Affection and love, combined with desire, exploded in their hearts, and they felt choked with emotion. Anna was completely lost in his embrace. What transpired between them, after that, was sacred. She felt that her cycle of life had achieved its completion. All she managed to whisper was, "I love you Sam. Thank you." This was the perfect moment and she wanted it never to pass. She closed her eyes. He whispered back, "I love you too, my darling lady." She smiled.

It was only three in the evening, but they fell asleep in each others' arms. Sam woke up first, at about six, and quietly went to make some coffee for both of them. Before leaving, he glanced at Anna and saw her sleeping so peacefully, with her mouth curved into an angelic smile and her hand on her chest. She looked so serene and beautiful...or was it because 'beauty is in the eye of the beholder?'

Sam found the coffee powder and the mugs without any problem. He had been to Anna's place years ago, and knew how organized she was. He made coffee and came back to wake her up. He felt so joyful, that he started whistling like a young boy as he entered her room. He suddenly stopped at the doorway, as his eyes fell on Anna. Something felt terribly amiss. She had not moved an inch, and her smile looked transfixed on her mouth. A chill ran through Sam. He ran to her side.

"Anna, wake up, my love," he almost screamed, but Anna did not move. There was neither breath nor heartbeat. He fell on her sobbing. Nothing upon Earth could have prepared him for this moment of excruciating pain and sorrow that pierced his heart. Dan, who was knocking at the door, heard the blood curdling cry of Sam, and entered with his spare key. Dan touched Anna's limp body and realized that it was too late. However, the smile on her face expressed nothing but peaceful joy and victory of love. As far as she was concerned, Love had won!

Her tombstone read,

Anna Grebowska

July 30, 1950 – September 15, 2011

"*This is one of the miracles of love: It gives a power of seeing through its own enchantments and yet not being disenchanted.*"

— C.S.Lewis

ACKNOWLEDGEMENTS

Special thanks go to my dear friend Don and an acquaintance, Ron, who were the first to encourage me to write this book. Thanks to `The Writers Union of Canada` and Anne Bougie at Johanna Bates Literary Agency, for their initial evaluation of my manuscript, which provided me with constructive criticism, guidance and advice. Thanks to Tim Plakolli and my account manager, Ceilidh Marlow, at FriesenPress, for going above and beyond their call of duty, to assist me with my every need, and to their editor for copy editing my manuscript.

I would also like to thank Ervad Nozer Kotwal for granting me an interview to discuss Zoroastrianism in depth, Mr. Behram Farsi for his insight into Zoroastrianism in Iran, and the many Parsis I met and befriended in the 'Bagh,' for their warmth and generosity of spirit in accepting me into their fold.

CPSIA information can be obtained at www.ICGtesting.com
Printed in the USA
LVOW11s0750181213

365758LV00001B/5/P